Co

Cover design by Donnie Goodman
Edited by Ben Long

THE ENDLESS AND OTHER STORIES

Brandon Baker

CONTENTS

AUTHORS NOTE

Thank you so much for choosing to read my first ever published work! I hope you have as much fun reading them as I did writing them. The following page contains content warnings for those that need them. Enjoy!

CONTENT WARNING

The Following Book Contains:

-Graphic violence and injury detail
-Mentions of self harming
-Stalking
-Brief mentions of animal harm
-Death of a loved one

To all of you, for encouraging me every step of the way.

UNBOTHERED

Corinne could still hear her neighbors screaming for their lives. The primal terror in their voices and deathly wails of unimaginable agony had long since lost their novelty, and she was starting to get a splitting headache. She finally found her noise-cancelling headphones, and their shrieking was thankfully snuffed out as she slipped them on. She just could not be bothered to care, let alone lend a helping hand.

She had tried to warn them, hadn't she? Multiple times, in fact. Had went door to door, showing them the video evidence that she had gathered, and vehemently tried to plead her case, doing her best to convince them that their lives were in danger. But they had all turned their backs on her, slamming the door in her face and humiliating her.

No one would talk to her in public anymore, but everyone talked about her. As soon as she walked by, all conversation would stop and all eyes would be upon her. Hostile, unfriendly. These people she had known all her adult life, treating her like a freak, a monster. Well, let them be slowly and mercilessly devoured by the *actual* monsters that she had tried to warn them about.

She pulled out her phone and looked at the time: 3:45 A.M. Only two hours and ten minutes until sunrise. She took off her sunglasses and cleaned them on her shirt, squinting her eyes against the blinding light shining throughout her home.

In every corner of every room in her two-story, colonial style house shone industrial-sized 1000-watt halogen freestanding lamplights. She had dozens of replacement bulbs, and if the power went out (as it was apt to do in the wintertime), she had ten hair-trigger floodlight flashlights capable of shining over 180,000 lumens and three totes filled with batteries – plus a last-ditch contingency plan, just in case. It was all extremely expensive, and her electric bill these past few weeks had been outrageous, but she knew they would come back, so it was worth the expense. At least she was saving on her heating bill.

She absentmindedly rubbed her arm, pausing for a moment over the charred concavity where a hunk of her forearm had been eaten away, shivering as she was struck by a wave of phantom pain. If they got her for good this time, it wouldn't be from a lack of trying on her part. She was ready for them.

Still on her phone, she tried pulling up the browser, but she hadn't had a signal since shortly after sunset, just right before her neighbors started screaming. She turned on her television, but every channel was static. She was tired of sitting around and doing nothing, so she pulled out the loveseat in her living room and began dusting, pausing to admire a picture of her and her late husband Carl on their wedding day. God, she missed him. It had been over five years since he passed, but every morning when she awoke she reached over to his side of the bed, expecting to feel his solid, reassuring warmth snoring softly beside her, and every morning reality came crashing down around her, a debilitating wave of sadness overwhelming her. If he was still here, he would have believed her in an instant. Not only because she had clear video evidence (not like those found footage bigfoot videos that looked like they were filmed with a potato), but because he trusted her entirely.

She set the photograph down carefully and quickly dusted behind the loveseat. She pushed it back against the wall, feeling a sharp twinge of pain in her lower back. Her contingency plan had taken a lot, almost all she had left in her, and now her whole body was exhausted and in horrible pain. She sat heavily on the couch, one arm slowly kneading her back muscles and the other mopping up the sweat on her forehead with the sleeve of her shirt. She accidentally jostled the headphones a bit and was hit with a sudden wave of sound from outside. The screaming hadn't abated in the slightest, and she could now hear what sounded like sticks being methodically snapped, along with a sound that, under different circumstances, could have been mistaken for wet cloth being torn into long strips.

Before readjusting her headphones, she heard the tinkling of breaking glass below her, instantly followed by an inhuman screeching, the sound like a million cars grinding up against a million guard rails. A moment later, there was the sound of more glass shattering and a flurry of movement, and the old wood basement door started shuddering in its frame as dozens of dark forms started ramming against it.

Fuck, Corinne thought grimly, *that happened sooner than I expected.* She hadn't been able to fortify the basement like she had the rest of the house. There weren't enough outlets in the basement, and she kept blowing fuses every time she tried to MacGyver it with various extension cords. She had an electrician coming Monday, but oh well.

She got up from the couch carefully, one arm still pressed into the small of her back and pointed a few of the floor lamps directly towards the basement door. She walked to the edge of the room, stopping at the landing leading upstairs, waiting, hearing only the sound of her blood echoing in her ears thanks to the headphones, when the familiar burnt-plastic-with-an-overtone-of-rot smell came to her.

The old door started to rattle wildly in its frame, and then a moment later it exploded inward in a shower of wood and dust, and standing at the precipice of the doorway was a wall of writhing darkness.

She knew if she took off her headphones she'd hear that

awful rending metal sound, so she didn't bother, but she took a few seconds to watch, entranced at the carnage below. It was impossible to see where one ended and the other began. Hundreds, maybe thousands of inky forms were frying under the powerful lights, held at bay for the time-being at the basement doorway. The walls of the basement stairwell was already stained an oil slick black as their nightmare bodies were melted away. The sight of them being incinerated was like heat emanating off blacktop on a scorching summer's day.

As fast as Corinne's aching body could manage, she ran back beside the couch, grabbing two of the flashlights off the end table at the bottom of the stairs. She quickly changed the settings to "Beacon" and shone the powerful spotlights on the squirming mass. The sounds of their death wails finally penetrated through her headphones, and every hair on her body stood on end, but she didn't let up, shining the blinding white light all over the gyrating pitch-black form of the shade-like monsters. She laughed, imagining that she looked like she was directing air traffic, and felt exhilarated from a wave of adrenaline.

Corinne felt vindicated watching the shade's hideous bodies disintegrate. She'd been plagued with terrible nightmares since she first encountered one of the creatures a few weeks back. She was walking on the nature trail at the edge of town like she did most early mornings, enjoying the peace and tranquility of the outdoors right before the sun came up, when she thought she saw movement. It was there and then gone, but Corrinne's curiosity was piqued, so she left the trail and walked deeper into the woods, searching for whatever it was.

The sun was just starting to rise, and the world was tinted a dark purplish color under the cover of trees, so she took out her phone and started recording, turning the flash on and pointing the camera around her, walking in circles. She was just about to turn around when she felt a sudden weight on her forearm, jerking her down and almost causing her to drop her phone, followed by an immense, searing pain.

She screamed, instinctively trying to swat whatever it was off her arm, but her hand met a strange, squishy resistance, and her palm felt like it was impaled by a thousand tiny needles. The pain was unlike anything she'd ever felt before, and she started flailing her arm about wildly, running out of the woods and back to the trail.

With each swing of her arm, she could see that it was coated in what looked like black tar. The pain felt like something was boiling her skin right off the bone. She remembered her phone and shone it on her arm, needing to know what the fuck was latched on to her. She recoiled at the hellish sight as an earsplitting shriek pierced her ears.

There was a black *something* wrapped around her forearm, roiling in the bright light of her phone. It was a thing of shadow, and its constantly shifting shape hurt her eyes when she tried to focus on one single part of its shade-like form. She watched, mesmerized, as the thing slowly disintegrated into thin air, screeching like buzzsaw. It was burning away into a noxious cloud under the light.

The shadow creature refused to let go, and even though it was now half its original size that it was, it wouldn't unlatch. It continued to pulse in rhythm with the intense pain she was feeling, feeding on her even as it quickly faded away.

With one final howl, it was gone, along with most of her forearm. She looked, slack-jawed, at the charred innerworkings of her arm – the tendons, veins, muscles and everything else stained a deep black – and promptly passed out. Moments later, she was found by a couple walking their dog and was taken via ambulance to the local hospital, where she received extensive skin graft surgery. She had tried to explain what happened to anyone that would listen, tried to warn them what was bound to come next.

She had always been one to trust her gut, and she *knew* that there were more of these things out there. The detectives that took her statement didn't believe her, even after seeing the video. You could see the fucking thing on her arm, clear as day, evaporating and screeching that awful wail, but they barely gave it a passing glance. She shoved the screen in their faces every time she saw them, but it was no use.

She was released a few days later, and that's when she started going door to door, showing the video to all her friends and neighbors, but again, no one believed her. Corinne had tried to tell them what was coming, showing them what happened to her arm. She told them that the light from her phone had killed it, but they didn't listen. They felt bad for her, pitied her, convinced that she'd finally lost it. She was now the crazy old widow who lived alone and had turned batty in her grief and isolation.

Corinne could tell by the looks in their eyes that they were convinced she'd somehow managed to dig a trench out of her arm herself and then made the whole crazy story up. She was hurt at first. Hurt more than she ever could have imagined, if she was being truthful. These were her friends, or at least she thought they were, and they treated her like a headcase. Yes, it was awful, but she didn't dwell on it. Couldn't dwell on it. Because she knew what was coming, she started preparing.

Now she laughed wildly as she extinguished the shadow creatures that had become the bane of her existence. It felt good to finally be doing something instead of living in fear. Honestly, she was almost glad that they had come. Now everyone would know that she wasn't insane, that she should have been taken seriously. That she was right.

Her laughter abruptly stopped as she saw another wave of shades pour into the top of the basement landing. Creature after creature came until it was like a tsunami of roiling shadowy death. The entire living-room was quickly consumed by a foul-smelling haze as the shades evaporated. She started coughing uncontrollably and noticed that the fog was so thick that the lights were being overwhelmed, unable to fully penetrate the nebulous dark.

She switched the two flashlights to "Floodlight" and set them at the bottom of the stairs, pointed right at the basement. The shades continued to hiss and screech as the intense light touched them. She quickly opened the closet at the base of the stairs and took out the rest of her flashlights, all eight, and quickly turned them on. The shades stood no chance, and within seconds the last of them were burned away to nothing. In a few minutes, even the black oily residue they left was burned away, and the only trace of their intrusion was the shattered remains of the basement door strewn across her living room. She gave a primal shout, feeling triumphant.

The whole house shook as something roared in response, and she was thankful she still had her headphones on, as she was sure her eardrums would have ruptured. She carefully walked to the front window, tiptoeing around the slivers of broken wood, and peeled the curtain back, feeling her momentary sense of triumph vanish in a flash.

Corinne's neighborhood was a large cul-de-sac with twenty-nine other houses in a giant circle. A small community garden and gazebo in the center of the space served as a neighborhood hangout. Now, a shade the size of a whale sat where the gazebo should have been. It was massive, and Corinne could see the path of destruction it had taken to arrive at its current position in front of her house; the pavement was disintegrating under the immense bulk where the creature sat.

It was like a black hole, sucking up and obliterating everything in its path, and it was slowly coming her way. The shade sensed her fearful gaze and roared once more, the window in front of Corinne's face splitting into a million spiderwebbed cracks before blowing inward and peppering her face with glass.

She stepped back, looking at her flashlights and floodlamps, and felt her spirits drop. She looked at her watch, seeing that it was five in the morning. Only an hour away from sunrise. *I was so close*, she thought with regret. She was hoping that she'd be able to make it until then so she could tell anyone who was alive that she was right, that she had tried to warn them. Now it didn't look like she would have the chance. Before she lost her nerve, she started putting her contingency plan into place.

She ran up the stairs, faster than she would have normally and feeling her back twinge with distaste, but it wouldn't be much longer. She reached the landing and felt the ground beneath her feet sway as the house shook from another mighty roar. Without hesitating, Corinne unscrewed the top of the first 30-gallon drum that had been sitting at the top of her stairs for weeks, and with all her might, putting her shoulder into it and screaming through the pain spasming through her body, she shoved it down the stairs. The whole bottom half of her body was drenched as the liquid sloshed heavily down, and the dizzying scent of gasoline almost made her pass out, but she bit her lip hard, bringing her back to the moment.

Corinne took the cap off the second drum, shedding her earphones and throwing them down the stairs, hit with a tidal wave of sound, but wanting to experience this final moment in all its glory. She took her husband's engraved lighter out of her pants pocket and thumbed the top off, her finger on the ignitor, waiting, her hand poised over the top of the second container of gasoline.

Getting the empty 30-gallon barrels up the stairs had been hard enough, but filling them was even more difficult. It had taken numerous trips to the gas station to fill up her small, 5-gallon can, her neighbors standing by watching her with suspicious eyes, but two days ago she had finally gotten enough gas to fill up both barrels. Just in time.

In her final moments, Corinne thought of her late husband Carl. He had passed tragically in a house fire. He was a volunteer firefighter, and had died trying to save a child from a three-story apartment complex that had erupted in flames due to some faulty wiring. Unbeknownst to him, the child had already escaped through her bedroom window and was hiding in shock under the neighbor's porch. The roof had collapsed in on Carl as he was frantically looking for the girl. What divinely shitty luck. She figured it was only right that she went out the same way.

God, she missed him. Missed him so much it caused a physical pain in her chest. The smile lines that perpetually creased his eyes and mouth from a life spent laughing, the mischievous twinkle that was ever-present in his eyes, the way she could lay there for hours cocooned in his warm embrace; whatever came next, she hoped she could experience even a fraction of that happiness again. At least it wouldn't be long now.

As she stood waiting, the house shook more intensely with each passing second, the sound of the goliath shade's approach drowning out the sounds of her neighbor's death-shrieks. There was a moment of silence before the front of her house was ripped away in one single swoop, sounding like the world itself was being torn apart. Corrine's body was pierced with what felt like hundreds of shards of shrapnel, and the floor beneath her feet shifted as the structure of her house tottered from the creature's attack. With a throat-splitting roar, Corrine thumbed the ignitor on Carl's lighter and the world went white.

CAT DAD

Dennis

It was a beautiful fall day. The sun was shining brightly, the leaves just starting to change colors, the morning air cool and crisp, when Dennis fell and twisted his ankle. He was walking in his spacious, fenced-in backyard, shaking a container of treats, calling out his cat's name, and was starting to get worried when he suddenly slipped on a patch of grass still damp with morning dew. The treat container went flying from his pinwheeling hands as he tried to correct his balance, but it was no use; his knees buckled and down he went, his right ankle folding beneath his weight, the ligaments tearing, the bones fracturing slightly, sending lightning bolts of pain shooting up his entire leg.

He immediately tried to stand, putting his full weight on the injured ankle, but with a sickening pop and another dizzying lance of pain, he fell once more, this time flat on his face. His chin connected with the ground and caused him to bite the inside of his cheek hard, the warm, coppery taste of blood filling his mouth.

He lay there for several moments, completely frazzled, wondering what the hell had just happened. He heard a faint chime of a bell and looked up to see his cat Babou pawing at the treat container, which now lay upside down in the grass several feet away. Dennis sighed, probing the inside of his torn cheek with the tip of his tongue and cringing at the feel of torn skin and the taste of more blood. He turned his head and spit, gagging at the taste, and looked back to find Babou standing about five feet away, staring at him in what could only be described as disgust. He deliberately turned his small head, refusing to acknowledge his existence. The cat then turned around with his tailed raised, giving Dennis an eye full of his feline ass, and ran quickly to the backdoor, where he stared up at the knob intently. He looked back at Dennis for a few beats with his eyes wide, as if to ask what the hell was taking so long, before turning his attention back to the door.

Dennis sighed once more and pushed himself up to a sitting position. He wanted to let Babou in quick before the cat ran off again, but he paused, sitting in the yard, the morning dew soaking his sweatpants. His ankle was throbbing with exponential pain, and before he lost his nerve, he pulled up the leg of his pants and stared, shocked.

In the few minutes since he fell, his ankle had already swelled to almost comical proportions. It looked like he'd been stung by a dozen bees. He couldn't even make out the hump of his ankle bone, it was so ballooned. The skin around it was an ugly blue-ish purple, and as he stared, he could swear it was getting bigger right before his eyes.

He felt in his pockets for his cell phone, but then remembered it was charging on the kitchen counter. He had been getting ready to go to the store when he realized that he hadn't seen Babou since the previous night, and after walking around the house shaking the treat container and looking in all the usual places (Dennis learned long ago that calling Babou's name was an exercise in futility, but he was sometimes motivated by food), he realized that the cat had somehow gotten out again.

Even though Babou acted indifferent to Dennis's very existence, Dennis couldn't imagine his life without the grumpy cat. Dennis didn't have any close family or any friends to speak of. He worked from home where he essentially input data from one spreadsheet to another, the only interactions with his co-workers and upper management coming in the form of companywide email correspondence. He barely even got any calls from telemarketers and paid all his bills online or over the phone with a robotic automated machine. Other than the occasional trip to the grocery store, or the even rarer trip to the movies, Dennis's only interaction with another living being was his 6-year-old, slightly overweight tabby cat.

Dennis frequently wondered what he would do if something happened to his only companion. His house was basically a cat's utopia. In every room, there were cat trees in varying sizes, various toys littering the floor, and cat beds in the corners and suction cupped to almost every window. He had installed little shelves on the walls where Babou could climb up and see the house from high vantage points, but Babou seemed to only use them to surprise attack Dennis, climbing to eye level and scratching him in the face (the frequency of these occurrences leading Dennis to believe that this might be Babou's favorite pastime). But no matter how much time or money Dennis invested into making Babou feel comfortable in the house, all Babou seemed to want to do was run outside.

Dennis wouldn't mind this so much if Babou just liked to lay out and sun himself and stayed close to the house. But no, the second Babou got out, he just disappeared, sprinting away from the house and throwing Dennis into near-hysterics, certain that something horrible would happen, and he would never see his beloved cat ever again.

Dennis had to let Babou in soon, before he ran off again. Mentally bracing himself, he planted both hands in the wet grass and pushed himself forcibly upward, shrieking shrilly as his injured ankle shifted, the pop of stretched ligaments and torn tendons sending tidal waves of pain throughout his whole body, black spots forming in front of his eyes.

Still balancing on one leg and with his hands spread out in a T on either side of him, Dennis couldn't help but laugh, imagining

THE ENDLESS AND OTHER STORIES

how ridiculous he must look. His laugh turned to a cry as his ankle rolled and he almost fell again. He gritted his teeth through the pain and started hopping his way back towards his home, where Babou impatiently waited, completely ignoring Dennis's painful cries.

With each hop on his good leg, Dennis's ruined ankle hung limply in the air, rolling wildly, the ligaments popping as they were stretched like taffy, the muscles tearing to shreds, and broken bones grinding together noisily. Dennis was out of his mind in pain and didn't stop to consider that maybe hopping wasn't the best strategy. He only had one thing on his mind: get to the door so he could let Babou inside, and then he would worry about himself.

Dennis had yet to realize that Babou had runoff the second Dennis's cries turned into incoherent shrieks of anguish and was now watching his owner cautiously from behind a tree. Dennis's vision was full of stars from the inconceivable agony, and he could only make out the vague outline of his backdoor, so he assumed Babou was still there.

After what seemed like an eternity, Dennis finally reached the backdoor. Still balancing on one foot, he fell forward with his hands braced outward, palms open, expecting to feel the reassuring solid oak of his back door, where he would rest a second to catch his breath, and if his vision was clear and straight, he might have. But he aimed too high, and instead of wood, his hands slapped hard against the glass window that was cut into the middle of the door. The momentum of his fall shattered the window, causing his arms to shoot through and tearing down the cat-adorned curtains on the inside with a clatter.

Miraculously, Dennis was left completely unscathed by the broken glass. He paused, panting and trying to clear his head, his damaged foot hanging by a thread and his rag-doll arms hanging limply through the busted window to his elbows, keeping him upright. The muscles in his uninjured leg hurt almost as much as his injured one and were burning fiercely from exertion.

After a few deep breaths, Dennis craned his head down to look at his foot and instantly regretted it, bile burning the back of his throat and causing the blackness to take over his vision once more.

His foot was swollen to almost three times its normal size. His skin had turned the color of almost ripe blackberries and was shining and taut, looking like it could rupture at any second. His toes were a dark grey color, and he couldn't feel them at all.

Now that Dennis thought about it, the pain was starting to abate, which was odd, but he could thankfully think a little more clearly. However, a strange cold sensation was starting to set in instead, as if he just plunged his foot into a bucket of ice water. Dennis did not take this as a good sign.

Dennis's weight was being mostly supported by his arms, the edge of the window frame cutting into the inside of his elbows painfully, as he thought of the best way to extricate himself. He was already starting to feel pinpricks in his fingertips as the blood rushed there, his arms in danger of falling asleep. He looked into his kitchen, spotting his cellphone lying on the island, still plugged into the charger. There was no way Dennis would be able to drive with his foot in its current state, so the phone was his only salvation. He thought about crawling through the now open window, but he could see some stray shards of glass sticking dangerously out of the frame and ruled out that idea.

Then he laughed, mentally kicking himself as he realized his stupidity; the back door was unlocked, all he had to do was pull his arms out carefully and turn the doorknob, then hobble inside. The morning light was illuminating the kitchen, and Dennis noticed with a start just how filthy the place was. A fine coating of dust and cat hair coated every surface, crinkle toys, empty cat food tins, and catnip-mouses littering the floor.

It was then that he remembered Babou, and looked wildly around, not seeing him anywhere. He called his name frantically, then calmed down and called his name in a more placating tone, but Babou was nowhere to be seen. Twin vice grips of panic took hold of Dennis's lungs, the world closing in around him as he imagined all the horrible things that could have happened to his beloved tabby. Quickly, gracelessly, Dennis yanked his left arm out of the window, the rough wood of the window frame scarping his skin raw, but he barely even registered the pain. He gripped the door handle firmly and used it as a support to keep him steady while he carefully removed his right arm.

His balance betrayed him, and he hopped back a few inches, turning the doorknob at the same time reflexively, and yanking his remaining arm from the window with a quick jerk. He felt a deep, icy slash of pain in his inner forearm. The next moment he felt hot wetness sheeting quickly down his arm and drenching his shirt and sweatpants, but he refused to look at the damage.

The knob still gripped in his hand, he yanked the door open and hopped back, letting it swing open and smack loudly against the side of the house, the rest of the glass in the window breaking and falling out. Dennis still refused to look down at his arm, but he could hear the sound his blood made as it pattered against the slab of sidewalk that served as his back porch, and the louder sharp tapping it made on the hardwood of his kitchen floor as he stumbled inside.

Dennis hopped through the kitchen, not caring that he was leaving a snail trail of bright red blood on the floor, and that with each body-flopping hop more blood flew from his limp right arm in a crimson shower. Dennis's vision was starting to go blurry around the edges, and his uninjured foot was now completely soaked and making a loud wet splat with each hop, but he was only a few feet away from his phone, a few short hops away from being able to call for help.

He was just within arm's reach and was grasping for the cellphone, when his foot landed directly on the top of an old cat food tin, causing his leg to fly out from beneath him. The sound of his head cracking against the hardwood floor sounded like a gunshot in the near silent morning.

Dennis awoke a few moments later, unsure of where he was at first, only aware of the sharp, stabbing pain in the back of his head. The world started registering, and he took notice of the cat hair and dust suspended in the air, disrupted from his fall, and the familiar sight of the old, water-stained drop ceiling of his kitchen.

He tried to move his legs but was reminded of his destroyed ankle with a wave of agony. His body felt wet and hot, like he had just finished a workout from one of the DVD's he ordered from the library, but he realized with a jolt that the metallic wetness he was smelling was not sweat, and he remembered what happened to his arm with another jolt of pain. The events of the morning came back to him in a flood, and Dennis started to sob, feeling overcome with self-pity. Excruciating pain radiated throughout his body, and he felt so spent and tired that when the blackness started to take over his vision again, he didn't fight it.

Dennis knew he was close to his phone, but decided in that moment, bleeding out on his kitchen floor and hurting from a dozen places, that he wasn't going to bother. Even if he called for help, what did he have to live for? Babou had run off and would probably never come back again. Dennis didn't blame him. Even if the tabby wasn't already lying dead in the woods or on the side of the road after being hit by a careless driver; from Babou's perspective on the back porch, Dennis had charged after him, screaming like a monster. He was certain he'd never see Babou again.

No, this was for the best. If Babou was lucky, he would make it to one of the neighbors' houses nearby, and they would take him in and be the owners that Babou deserved. Dennis was selfish for thinking he could ever own such a magnificent creature as Babou, for thinking he deserved him. He lay there in an ever-growing puddle of his own blood, crying silently, as he waited for the darkness to overtake him for good.

Babou

Babou had spent a *lovely* morning outdoors. He had snuck out the previous night when The Man was retrieving the pizza box another Man had left on the front step, running stealthily into the night without either of The Men knowing, which was just great.

Nights were always scary for Babou, and he would jump at every crunch of leaves and snapping of sticks, but it was always worth it for the morning. He would sit at his customary spot on a low hanging branch of a crab apple tree (The Man had yet to discover his spot, which delighted Babou to no end) and watch the world wake up. By the end of the night, Babou would always be so depleted, his energy spent and his nerves fried, but the second the sun's glorious rays lit up his even more glorious fur, he immediately felt a second wind wash over him. The world was a better place come sunrise. The monstrous shadows dissipated, every noise suddenly sounding much less menacing, and the leaves and grass twinkling with a million dewdrop diamonds.

Babou was about to start rolling around on the concrete when The Man came outside screaming his head off, yelling Babou's name over and over again in varying degrees of desperation, his grating voice making Babou's skin *crawl*. The Man just couldn't live unless he was souring Babou's mood.

Babou enjoyed watching The Man for a bit and was tempted to come when The Man went inside and came back out shaking the treat container, but then The Man fell.

This interested Babou because it had never happened before, and the sound of The Man's shouts changed from the usual nails on a chalkboard to something that worried Babou in a way he didn't quite understand.

He went over to investigate, carefully treading through the wet morning grass to where The Man lay prone and moaning. His attention was diverted when he noticed the treat container lying in the grass and decided that was much more interesting than The Man could ever hope to be.

After trying in vain to gain access to the mouthwatering treats, Babou grew frustrated and decided to see what The Man was going on about. He crept cautiously towards him, when suddenly The Man turned and spit *right at Babou.* Babou was both appalled and disgusted, and made sure to relay that message by flattening his ears and showing The Man his behind.

He ran quickly towards The Prison and sat on the concrete, staring pointedly at the door then back at The Man, willing him to hurry up so he could piss on The Man's pillow. Babou was happy to see The Man get up, but he was screaming something awful now, at a register that threatened to crack Babou's head right open. Babou didn't understand The Man at all, but he knew enough to know that something was seriously up, and he needed to get away to safer grounds to better assess the situation.

He ran away from the back door and safely hid behind a tree to wait for things to calm down. Things didn't calm down, as The Man's screaming hardly abated in the slightest, and just as Babou was about to run off, maybe to find another Prison with another Man, the screaming stopped, followed by a loud breaking sound that was like music to Babou's ears (one of his favorite hobbies was pushing fragile objects off of high ledges and listening to the splendid crashing noise - this was like that), and then the back door to The Prison was open and The Man was inside.

Babou was relieved and made his way back home. Halfway there, he heard another loud noise, and then silence. Babou froze, but then resumed walking when he heard the familiar sound of The Man crying. The Man stopped making noise again just as Babou reached the back deck and noticed the blood on the ground. It was everywhere, and Babou crinkled his nose at the unexpected smell. He was about to run back to his crab apple tree when he noticed The Man lying on the floor, in more blood. A lot of it.

Babou didn't have much of a kill drive, but he wasn't opposed to hunting the occasional mouse or bird, and he associated blood with his infrequent hunts. Blood was the smell of death, so it confused Babou very much to see The Man lying in so much of it.

Did that mean The Man was dead? Babou didn't know, but even though he wasn't particularly fond of The Man or his numerous asinine rules, the thought of The Man being dead sent a feeling of dread down Babou's spine and up his tail.

He carefully picked his way through the kitchen, trying his best to avoid the blood but finding it impossible to avoid all together, and jumped on The Man's chest.

He waited, meowing loudly and panicking when he got no response. Babou purred and made the *bbbrrrppt* noise that always drove The Man crazy, but again got no response.

He crawled up The Man's chest and studied his face, not knowing what else to do. It seemed like The Man was really gone, and with a sorrowful yowl, Babou went up to The Man's face and started licking his salty, tear-streaked cheeks. Babou didn't quite have the capacity to express exactly what he was feeling, but he wanted to say goodbye to The Man that had taken care of him.

They might not have seen eye to eye all the time (or ever), but Babou could always feel how much The Man loved him, and that made Babou realize he loved The Man too, in his own begrudging way.

Babou nearly jumped out of his skin when he felt the fingers gently caressing his back, and he dug his claws into The Man's fleshy chest, ready to make his escape, when he heard The Man say his name in a weak voice he almost didn't recognize.

Babou purred like a motor, his eyes squinting, happy that The Man, *his* Man was still alive, and that he didn't actually have to go out and find a new one. That would have been an endeavor of epic proportions, and Babou was starving after his nighttime excursion.

He leaped off of The Man's chest, his usual disdain for The

Man returning now that he realized he was alive. Babou meowed loudly and ran over to his food bowl while The Man slowly, loudly made his clumsy way to the kitchen island, in the *exact opposite* direction of his food bowl.

Babou briefly contemplated running out of the still open back door as The Man went to his phone and started squawking away, but then he changed course, running quickly to The Man's bedroom to piss on his pillow instead.

BEAUTIFUL

Silas was in love. Real, heart-stopping, soul-enamoring, destiny-fulfilling love. His name was Will. He collects rocks and minerals and is always wading in the creek near his house looking for geodes, although he's yet to find one. He worked out seven days a week, almost exclusively climbing the indoor rock wall; the way he was able to scale it was truly a sight to behold. He dreamed of owning a farm one day, regardless of the fact that he was allergic to pollen and his fair skin burned even when it's cloudy. He was tall, easily six and a half feet, with a wiry, lanky build. His dark brown hair was easily mistaken for black until it hit a patch of light, then it resembled the deepest, most decadent chestnut. Will's facial features were what, individually, could be considered unconventionally attractive: small almond shaped eyes set a bit too close together, a crooked nose, slightly bucked teeth and small lips giving him an overbite, and a weak chin, but somehow, it all came together in an intriguing way, something you just couldn't look away from. Something truly unique.

Will works as a law clerk under the county district attorney, frequently acting as second or third chair, cross-examining witnesses and the accused. But he had his eyes set on the assistant prosecutor position, and one day, county prosecutor. Silas believed Will was shooting too low, and thought he easily had what it took to become the district attorney himself. Silas had seen what he could do in court, the verbal gymnastics he was able to perform and the effortless way he enraptured everyone in the courtroom with his words. His voice, a powerfully deep baritone, demanded your attention. Silas had experienced firsthand the kind of magic Will was capable of in a courtroom. That was where they had met, and it was love at first sight.

Silas had been about to give up on life before then. He was being held at the county jail awaiting trial for a complete misunderstanding, and he didn't see much merit in living in such a cruel, confusing world. Silas thought he had found the love of his life, but he had been tricked, and now in the eyes of the law he was a criminal.

Silas had gone against his court appointed lawyer's advice and had testified himself, vehemently defending his actions and trying to convince the judge that *he* was the victim, not that fucking deceptive rat *Toby*. Toby claimed that he suspected someone was breaking into his house after finding his possessions moved slightly or missing all together, so he set up a few hidden cameras. Toby didn't find any proof on the camera footage, but claimed he still felt convinced someone was breaking in and invading his privacy. He claimed that he didn't feel safe in his own home, and was starting to lose his mind, when his neighbors across the street called 911 after seeing Silas sneaking around the back of Toby's house. Toby, who had been jerked awake from a deep sleep at the sound of the doorbell ringing, started screaming when he saw Silas standing in the doorway of his bedroom. Silas had tried to explain, pleading with Toby to calm down and listen to reason, but Toby wouldn't, and instead started pummeling Silas despite his pleas. It didn't take long for the police to break down the front door, and Silas was taken away in handcuffs. It was all just a complete misunderstanding.

No, Silas was the victim and had tried to explain as much himself under oath. How could Toby be afraid for his life, but consistently leave the rear basement storm window unlocked? Why, when installing his cameras, did he leave his blinds open so Silas could watch the whole thing, seeing exactly where Toby "secretly" hid the cameras? And most importantly of all, why did Toby stare deeply into Silas's eyes every morning and ask how he was as Silas served him his breakfast at the university café where he worked, and where Toby was a professor?

Toby wasn't like the rest of those uppity fucks and spoiled brats who never gave Silas the time of day, who wouldn't even acknowledge his existence beyond giving him their breakfast demands. The sincerity in his voice and the yearning in his eyes while he addressed him still took Silas's breath away when he thought about it for too long. Toby wasn't like everyone else, who asked questions without wanting to know the answers. They shared a connection, and Silas tried to convince everyone in court of this fact. At one point, in a fit of desperation, Silas begged Toby to look at him, to please tell the court the truth and to stop playing these mind games, but Toby wouldn't look up, and Silas was threatened with being held in contempt of court.

Shortly after, the court had adjourned for lunch, and Silas was taken away to a holding cell in the courthouse where he was served a cold lunch meat sandwich. He feverishly worked on scraping the thick, clear plastic knife he was given against the bumpy concrete floor of the cell so he could slit his wrists wide open. He imagined how great it would be for all this to be over, cringing at the humiliation he just endured, but looking forward to how he would dig the plastic into his wrist to the fucking hilt and viciously saw through the bundles of veins and vital arteries until he couldn't anymore. The thought of it was making his mouth water, and he frantically scraped harder, but then stopped.

Silas was still going to kill himself, the thought of dying didn't really bother him, but what gave him pause was Toby. Silas was a realist. He knew that he had failed to convince the judge that what he said was true, that *he* was the victim. Toby had not only led Silas on, but now he was going to ruin his life by spreading lies, and he couldn't even look Silas in the eyes while doing it? Somehow, Toby had managed to brainwash the judge just like he had Silas. There was no doubt that Silas would go to jail. But how was it fair that someone as deceptive, manipulative, and just plain evil as Toby be allowed to walk this earth for one more second?

How many more hearts would he break, how many more lives would be ruined?

Silas resumed his scraping with renewed vigor, his body humming at the thought of plunging the blade deep into Toby's traitorous throat before turning the blade on himself. It wouldn't be the first time he'd killed, but it would unfortunately be the last. It would be worth it though to see the look on Toby's face. Yes, Toby would die drowning in his own blood with the understanding that *no one* fucked with Silas. No one.

When the knife was filed to a fine point, Silas pricked his hand, the tip of the sharp plastic sliding easily into his flesh and digging into the meat of his palm, but then quickly withdrew the blade so as not to cause too much bleeding. He heard the heavy footsteps, jangling keys, and raspy breathing that indicated the idiot guard's approach, and slid the weapon into the elastic waist band of his county jail-issued pants, quickly sucking the blood away from his palm. Silas pushed the lunch tray into the corner of the cell with his foot and stood against the far wall, waiting for the guard to unlock his cell and escort him back to court. The guards hadn't searched him since his initial arrest, but if this particular dumbass decided to, it would be the last thing he ever did. Silas was going to put Toby down.

Or at least he had planned to, but upon returning to the courtroom and being sworn back in, Silas was struck dumb by the presence of someone new. The man introduced himself as Will Hart. He explained that the prosecutor and assistant prosecutor were called away on an emergency, and with granted permission from the judge, he would be continuing Silas's cross examination. Silas was barely able to focus, having to remind himself to breathe and straining to keep his mouth from hanging open. Never had he seen a more beautiful, intriguing person. Silas found himself cowering under Will's intense scrutiny, intimidated by his unique beauty, and gave mumbled comments and non sequiturs in reply to Will's questioning. Silas was frequently asked by the judge to speak up or to give definitive answers, but he couldn't control himself.

Will ended his questioning and Silas was excused to go sit by his lawyer, Kevin or something. Maybe-Kevin tried asking Silas what the hell that was, but Silas didn't even acknowledge his existence; he couldn't keep his eyes off Will. Toby was completely forgotten; that worthless fucking pissant wasn't worth the effort it would take to kill him, and he certainly wasn't worth Silas's own life. Silas sat mesmerized, watching as Will gave his closing statements. It went by in a blur, but at the end Will turned towards Silas and pointed at him, their eyes locking for a moment, and Silas felt *something* pass between them.

In that moment, Silas saw Will's eyes flash. They were an enchanting hazel, but for a second they seemed to look completely black, an endless, all-consuming void. There was a loneliness there, and a disdain for the world that Silas had only seen within himself. The moment passed when Will blinked, his eyes returning to their mesmerizing color, but the feeling remained, like a puzzle piece fitting together. A feeling of kinship, that he wasn't alone in this world. This wasn't like Toby, or any of the other dozens of past failed conquests – this was real. This was something worth fighting for. Worth *dying* for. Silas would stop at nothing until Will was his, forever.

Silas was found guilty of one charge of misdemeanor breaking and entering, the only charge they could definitively prove, and he was sentenced to the maximum sentence of one year imprisonment. Silas kept his head down, biding his time for the moment he could see Will again, imagining that Will was plagued with similar thoughts about Silas, and with good behavior he was out in nine months. He was on probation, with strict instructions not to go within a thousand feet of Toby, but that wouldn't be a problem. Silas thought long and hard in prison about what he would do with Toby, ultimately deciding that he would do nothing, at least not anytime soon. If the opportunity arose, Silas would be sure to take it, but he contented himself by knowing that Toby's days were numbered. In the meantime, Silas was now free to pursue Will, and he was determined not to fuck things up this time.

Silas made sure to stay within the guidelines of his probation; he showed up promptly to the part time job he had secured at the laundromat near his house, didn't go out past his curfew (at first), and made sure he was early to his appointments with his probation officer. Every other free moment of his life was spent tracking Will and accounting for his movements.

It took a few weeks for Silas to feel fully comfortable with Will's daily routine, but he eventually felt sure enough that he could follow Will with his eyes closed. Silas awoke at 4 A.M. and drove the fifteen minutes to Will's home, which he was able to find easily by looking on the county auditor's page. Will owned a single story 1200-square-foot ranch style home in a suburb located in a slightly impoverished part of town, which Silas thought was odd considering he worked for the district attorney and could surely afford nicer accommodations, but Silas figured Will liked the relative solitude. There were woods bordering the house to the left, and the house neighboring his to the right and the one across the street looked have been vacant for some time. Silas was able to park up the street in front of another vacant house and hide a few feet in the woods, unseen. He still had a pretty clear view of Will's home, but had never actually seen inside. Despite the pair of high-power binoculars he'd found at the military surplus store years ago, the most he saw was the occasional flutter of curtains as Will moved about.

If Will had an alarm clock Silas couldn't hear it, but every morning Will was out the door at 4:45 sharp to get to the gym at 5. Silas would run on the treadmill while Will scaled the thirty-foot climbing wall. Climbers were required to wear a safety harness, but the worker supervising the wall would let Will go without one, everyone staring in awe as he scaled the wall with ease, his slim form almost a blur as he practically flew to the top.

After an hour at the gym, Will would return home. Silas would watch stealthily from the trees until Will was out the door again at seven to make the forty-five-minute commute to the district attorney's office. Silas typically worked mornings and had just enough time to get to his shift at the laundromat by eight. It was usually dead, and Silas would spend his free time scouring the internet for any shreds of information he could find about Will, but there wasn't much. He had absolutely no social media presence, and when you googled his name there were only a handful of articles that popped up in relation to a few cases he'd worked on. Other than that, there was nothing. It was strange to not have any online presence in this day and age; Will truly was an enigma, and that made Silas hungrier to find out more.

Silas considered driving into the city to see Will get off work, but ultimately decided against it. The district attorney's office was located in the heart of downtown, only a few blocks away from his previous employer and the college that Toby still worked at (Silas was still friends with Toby on Facebook, weirdly enough, and saw that he had recently tricked the administration into thinking he was deserving of a grant to continue his research, which was bullshit in Silas's humble opinion). It wasn't worth violating his probation if Toby saw Silas passing by and called the police.

Will would come home at around seven in the evening, looking disheveled from his long day and the rush hour traffic, and would stay there for the rest of the night. He spent a lot of time on his back patio, staring out into the woods with a thoughtful expression on his face. It was fall, and the air would get quite chilly in the evenings, but he seemed to like the cold. Silas wondered if Will felt him out there in the woods, if he could feel his overpowering love and adoration, and decided that he must. There were many times when Will seemed to be looking directly at Silas, and he had to physically restrain himself from charging out of the woods and proclaiming his undying love. But it was much too soon for that. He had to settle for staying back and soaking in Will's otherworldly appearance from a distance, his pale skin seeming to glow in the dying light, his eyes looking black and featureless like that fateful day in the courtroom.

On the weekends Will would still go to the gym in the morning, but he seemed to like to spend most of his time outdoors. He would walk from his home and down a well-used path in the woods with a pair of rubber galoshes slung over one bony shoulder, wearing a wide brimmed sun hat. Will's destinations on these weekend jaunts was a beautiful, crystal clear creek about 10 minutes away from his house, and he would wade in the knee-high water, bent at the waist at an almost 90-degree angle for hours at a stretch. Silas would stare through his binoculars from a safe distance, mesmerized. He wondered what Will could be doing, fascinated that he could hold that position for so long.

During Will's third outing to the creek, Silas came to the conclusion that he was looking for geodes or river rocks, and probably had a collection in his house (Oh what he wouldn't do to see that collection. My god, he couldn't wait *just couldn't fucking wait*). He was proven wrong when Will's arm shot out quick as lightening, the suddenness of the movement causing Silas to drop his binoculars. He hurriedly grabbed them up, and when he put them back into position his heart almost stopped. Will was staring in his direction, mouth so agape that his jaw must surely be unhinged from its socket, his eyes jet black. Gripped in his hand, so hard his fingers looked to be breaking through its skin, was a large carp, unmoving. Silas fled, feeling exhilarated.

Silas had decided while in prison not to make his presence known to Will until the time was right. This was not out of the ordinary; he'd had to pine after many of his previous loves in secret, but Will was the type of love that comes once in a lifetime, and he was *not* going to fuck it up. Silas knew that he was the one; he had felt the connection that day in court, knew that Will had to have felt it too, but Silas had learned long ago that he couldn't just walk up to him, proclaim his undying love and tell him they were destined to be together forever. These things required a bit of finesse, and at times, a little convincing (which sometimes got ugly), but he would know when the perfect opportunity arose.

This went on for weeks, and Silas learned a lot about his future life partner. Will kept a strict routine, always stuck to the same unwavering schedule. Seven days a week he would climb at the gym. Monday through Friday he would work, and in the evenings he would sit outside before heading in for the night. Except for the gym, weekends were spent exclusively outdoors, rain or shine, either wading in the creek for fish or climbing trees with the same agility he exhibited at the climbing wall. Silas could never get close enough to see what he was doing in the trees, but they shook ferociously as he climbed. Sometimes Silas could hear birds squawking in fright before the noise was suddenly snuffed out, and he assumed Will was looking for eggs or maybe catching birds somehow with his bare hands like he did with the fish. His athleticism was remarkable.

Silas never once saw Will shop for groceries. He assumed Will probably ate his meals at work since he was so busy, and his weekend activities must have provided enough sustenance to hold him over outside of work hours. Silas thought that was a reasonable enough assumption to make, but when they were finally together, he would be sure to provide the meals for the both of them. Will was just so dreadfully thin, but thankfully, Silas loved to cook. He imagined they would buy a farm together and raise their own livestock so they could live off the land. Silas thought Will would appreciate that.

Silas would often daydream of his life with Will. Beautiful, hopeful dreams of their future together. He dreamt of the farm they would buy together, one with a pond and a river so they could fish, and with a beautiful, forested mountain vista in the distance, one they would climb together. In these reveries, Silas would encourage Will to become the district attorney, and Will would know that together, he and Silas could accomplish anything.

Silas also had vivid, terrifyingly realistic nightmares where Will not only rejected him, but publicly humiliated him and made a mockery of his love. These dreams left Silas gasping awake, soaked in a cold sweat and feeling both miserable and scared shitless in equal measure.

At work, Silas imagined he saw Will everywhere. Hiding amongst the detritus in the storage room, just rounding the corner or walking out the door after Silas was done helping a customer. But every time he ran to see if it was really him, there was never anyone there. The feeling of having *just missed* him remained, and it was starting to drive Silas mad.

Silas prided himself on being a reasonable man, on always taking things slow with potential lovers and never rushing; these things required finesse after all, but Silas knew he wouldn't be able to wait much longer. Will was special, Silas already knew that, but this feeling, this yearning, this *need*, was unlike anything Silas had ever felt before. He would need to make the next step, and soon.

Silas was barely sleeping anymore, and when he did it was a light, restless sleep filled with horrific nightmares. He hadn't shown up for work in over a week, and his parole officer was leaving threatening messages that Silas barely listened to. One night, sixty-one days after getting out of prison and following Will daily, sixty-one days of really getting to know him and observing his activities with a loving eye, Silas decided that it was time he broke into Will's home.

Silas had never waited so long to confess his feelings before, and he couldn't wait to take their relationship to the next level any longer. He was getting careless, waiting outside Will's house all night, hoping for a glimpse inside. Sometimes he'd even go as far as to walk right up to his house, trying like mad to get a peek behind the heavy blackout curtains that covered every window, but he still hadn't managed to get even the slightest view of what

Will's home looked like. Every now and then he'd hear a strange noise, almost like a sorrowful moaning followed by a piercing buzzing sound that made him cover his ears, but nothing else.

Silas waited five minutes after Will left for the gym before quickly emerging from the woods, making a beeline for the rear of Will's home. Wasting no time, he took out a lock pick kit from his jacket pocket and went to work. After only a few moments he stopped, confused. He hesitated, then turned the doorknob, stupefied when the door opened inward. The door was unlocked. Had it always been? He slowly stepped inside, eyes adjusting to the bright florescent lights that were left on, and he was again struck dumb – the house was empty.

The home consisted of a single-story open floor plan with old, worn, hardwood flooring. Directly in front of the backdoor was the kitchen-area, which had laminate tile, plenty of counter space, and room for appliances, but there was nothing. The rest of the house looked just as vacant. There was no couch or TV or washer or dryer or anything a person would expect to find in a home, save for a large square area rug in the center of the room. Where Silas was standing, he could see a bedroom down a hall to his left and a bathroom adjacent to that.

Silas closed the door behind him and walked further into the house, his footsteps echoing loudly. He quickly checked the bedroom and bathroom but found nothing in either. No pictures on the wall, no bed in the bedroom, just...nothing. Silas noticed that there was a fine layer of dust on the toilet, sink, and the porcelain claw foot tub in the bathroom, as if none had been used in sometime. He walked back into the main room, trying to wrap his head around what he had seen, when he was struck by an idea. He quickly walked over to the edge of the area rug.

Crouching down, he swept the rug aside and was only vaguely surprised to see a hole cut into the floor. He was shocked though when he took out his flashlight and shone it down the hole and he couldn't see the bottom, not even close. His flashlight was high powered and very expensive, but the light wasn't strong enough to permeate the darkness within the pit, not by a long shot. Silas quickly went outside, grabbed a handful of gravel from Will's back patio, and then chucked it down the hole. He waited two whole minutes and didn't hear it hit the bottom, which Silas had to admit was pretty odd.

Suddenly Silas heard a clicking noise behind him and turned around, his blood running cold at the sight of Will standing in front of the backdoor. As Silas watched, Will reached behind his back and twisted the lock.

He was still dressed in his workout clothes, his long, emaciated arms and stick-like legs hairless and smooth, perfect. It was bitingly cold in the house, an incessant, frost-like breeze seemed to be emanating from the hole, but it didn't seem to bother Will. He smiled at Silas, his buck teeth poking out of his small, bright red puckered lips. Silas smiled back, blushing furiously, looking down and crossing his arms, holding himself, wishing he could disappear.

Silas didn't know what to do. His heart was beating out of his chest and his mouth had gone dry. This wasn't how things were supposed to go. He mumbled an apology and was trying to think of what else to say when Will pressed a hand to Silas' chest, stopping him in his tracks. Silas gasped and tried to step back, but he was frozen in place. Will's hand was astonishingly cold, and an icy burn spread deep within Silas's chest. He started to panic, barely able to breathe, screaming internally, his mind demanding his body to run, but he couldn't move an inch.

Silas's eyes inched ever so slowly over Will's body, the effort taking every last bit of strength he had left, until they reached the pitch black, featureless orbs that were Will's eyes. They were terrifying, endless chasms, devoid of light, much like the pit in his living room – and they were beautiful. The most beautiful things Silas had ever seen. He imagined he could see shapes swirling around in that blackness, the limitless depth of them both unsettling and enticing, something Silas wouldn't mind getting lost in forever.

Still holding his hand to Silas's chest, Will whispered, "I've been waiting for you."

His voice seemed to come from all directions, ringing through Silas's head like a tolling bell and melting his heart. Then the cold enveloped Silas's lungs and his breathing stopped. He blacked out shortly thereafter.

Silas awoke sometime later still unable to move, feeling a strange tugging sensation on his left arm, followed by a loud crack and a sound not unlike corn being shucked. He tried to reach out, tried to turn his head and investigate, but couldn't. He also couldn't feel anything except the deep chill and the odd pulling sensation. With a tremendous effort he opened his eyes to slits, temporarily blinded by a harsh fluorescent light.

Silas was in the bathtub, staring up at a dripping shower head. He couldn't feel the water tapping on his skin, couldn't feel his body at all and had no control over his extremities, but knew that something was shaking him like a rag doll. His body felt heavy and useless, like his consciousness was somehow placed inside a mannequin.

The smell was odd, metallic and familiar somehow. The sounds were horrendous: wet smacking and meaty chewing, followed by an almost cartoonish gulping. It halted for a second, and Silas saw a grotesquely skeletal hand coated to the wrist in red slide across his vision and pull his eye lids closed, followed by an alien, insectile buzz that to Silas sounded like a laugh. There came a new sound, almost like someone squeezing a handful of Vaseline through clawed hands; a gelatinous, squelching noise.

It took him even longer to open his eyes this time, as they were now sticky and coated with red gore, and when he did the world was tinted crimson. His head was tilted at a downward angle so instead of seeing the dripping shower head, he came face to face with Will, except it wasn't the same man Silas had been pining after, not him at all.

His eyes were the size of dinner plates, extending all the way to his hairline and covering where his nose and cheeks should have been, and they were black as night, seeming like they were absorbing the light. His mouth spanned ear to ear and was filled with hundreds, maybe thousands of needle-sharp, hooked teeth pointed in every direction, scraps of torn flesh, grisly red chunks, and clear snail-like slime caught in the points and crevices. He was naked, his emaciated form bone white and glowing in the harsh fluorescents, his stomach obscenely concave with no belly button, every rib standing in stark relief against his taught skin. There was no sex between his legs, the skin there smooth and blemish-less, like a Ken doll.

Silas tried to speak, but all that came out was a pitiful exhale. Will cocked his head with a sharp jerk, movement seeming to stir and swirl in his limitless eyes. He gently caressed Silas's bare chest with taloned fingertips and feeling suddenly came rushing back to Silas, overwhelming his senses. He took a deep breath of foul-smelling air, his head swimming from the sudden rush of oxygen.

"You're beautiful," Silas gasped. "Thank you for choosing me." He looked down at his arm, unsurprised to see that it now ended in a bloody stump just above where his elbow was supposed to be. The stump was covered in a clear gelatinous slime, and he felt no pain whatsoever, just pleasant tingling.

"You're beautiful," Silas repeated, in awe of the creature before him. Silas stared into the depths of the Will-Thing's eyes, not seeing a single fleck of iris or color, not a single imperfection, only abysmal, divine, limitless darkness. Silas saw himself in his eyes, felt a kinship there. This was not exactly what Silas had in mind when he was yearning after Will, but maybe this wasn't so bad. Silas wondered if he'd get to see inside the hole in Will's floor, but it didn't matter one way or the other. Will had chosen Silas, and Silas couldn't have been happier. He started crying, tears of joy mixing with the blood on his face.

Will started to close the distance between them, leaning his nightmarish, perfect face towards Silas, his jaw unhinging, his infinite teeth seeming to rotate. Silas moaned with pleasure as Will resumed feeding, blacking out frequently from the pain, but awaking moments later and repeating in a gargling voice, "You're beautiful, thank you, you're beautiful, thank you, you're beaut–"

THE ENDLESS

1

It's been four weeks since you were taken, three days since I last tried to bring you back, two hours since I got off the phone with Detective Reynolds, and five minutes since I decided to end things. It took a while, but eventually I calmed down, my body sore from sobbing and weak from hunger. I hadn't been able to eat since you left me for good, and I knew I couldn't go on much longer. That I wouldn't. I had tried explaining to Reynolds one last time that it was just a matter of will, that if only I could focus *just right* I could break through the veil again like the night you were taken, and I could somehow find you and pull you back through. But as always, he wouldn't listen, saying nothing and letting the silence linger, which said everything. *She's lost it, her grief has consumed her, what has she done?*

Before hanging up, Detective Reynolds said that he didn't want me going out there anymore. That he didn't want me to spend any more time alone. He asked if there was someone I could maybe stay with, or at the very least if there was someone I could talk to. I lied and said that my friends were with me, I was never alone. I could tell he didn't believe me, that he knew I didn't have any friends. I know he's had me under 24-hour surveillance since you were taken, that he's followed me every night to your campsite, that he's become obsessed with finding out what happened to you, his obsession rivaling mine. Had he not seen what happened to me the night we discovered the site where you were taken? But that was unimportant now. I would go back tonight, one final time. I would either find a way to bring you back, or I would fail again. One way or another it would end tonight.

2

You had been on a solo camping trip in the state park. This wasn't out of the ordinary, as you spent almost every waking moment outdoors, but you'd never visited this particular spot before. We were at the gas station filling up when an outdoorsy couple in an SUV pulled up to the pump next to us. You overheard them talking about the spot and quickly made friends, as you always do, and they told you all about it, how unique it was, how secluded and otherworldly. I stayed in the car but overheard the whole thing, and when you hopped in beside me, I could tell by the glint in your eyes that you were going, that you had to experience it for yourself. You went that very evening and have been gone ever since.

I was lying in bed, trying to read but mostly worrying about you, when your shadow came to me, along with a strange pressure in the center of my head. It was not uncomfortable, not like a headache or head cold. It was peculiar but oddly comforting. A sudden calm washed over me, along with a flood of knowledge at what I needed to do. There were no words, only feelings and a series of premonitions and revelations:

You had been taken from your campsite.

There was an impossible amount of blood.

Your body would never be found, not in this world.

I was the only one that could save you.

I was never one to think clearly in stressful situations; I quickly fell to pieces and went to you, for you always knew what to do. I tried to center your shadow in my line of vision, but you were always out of sight, always flitting away the second my eyes were to lay upon your dark, phantasmagoric form.

I was ready to grab my car keys and head to your campsite, when you darted in front of my eyes, the pressure in my head intensifying slightly, and I knew I had to report you missing. If I were to go missing, no one except you would notice. I had no friends, no family, no job to go to or coworkers; I wasn't like you. You would be missed, and there would be questions. So, without another thought, I called 911.

I lied, hysterically telling them you called me in a panic, saying that you told me where you were and to get help before you were cut off. I told them there were sounds of a struggle and you screamed before the call went dead and that I was worried for your safety. Minutes later, four uniformed officers and a plain-clothed, well-built man who introduced himself as Detective Reynolds came to our home to take my story.

I repeated what I told the dispatcher: that you called me begging for help, that it sounded like someone had attacked you, and that I was worried. I tried to replicate my hysterical tone on the 911 call, but I found myself recounting the story in a flat voice. I knew that this looked ingenuine, and the accusatory way they looked at me confirmed that, but I wasn't especially troubled. I still felt you with me, the strange pressure in my head pulsing slightly like an oddly comforting mental embrace. You were taken, and it was probably awful, probably the worst thing that could possibly happen to someone, but all I had to do was bring you back. This was just a formality.

I could tell they didn't buy my story, and I didn't blame them. I knew how I sounded, but I refused to tell them where you were taken, insisting that I come along as well. They made me call your phone multiple times, but of course you didn't pick up. I showed them the texts you had sent me hours before, the only proof I had that you actually went to the park, and Reynolds seemed to come around. He excused himself, saying that he had to make a few calls but would be right back. I sat impatiently with the four policemen, not saying anything, willing Reynolds to come back so we could leave. Just as I started to feel the panic coming on again, you flashed across my eyes, the force in my head thrumming, and I calmed down.

Detective Reynolds came back shortly after, and with some thinly veiled threats about the consequences of falsifying a police report and wasting police resources, he said we would go to see if we could find your campsite. We took the thirty-minute trip to the state park, me riding shotgun in Reynolds's unmarked car. Two cruisers with their lights strobing followed closely behind. I guided Reynolds to the state park, not needing GPS even though it was the dead of night, pouring rain, and I had never been there before. You were there with me, whispering wordless directions in my head the whole way there.

3

In between following my directions, Reynolds peppered me with questions: *How long have you known Miss Nguyen?* Since 8th grade, and her name's Bea. *How long have you been a couple?* Unofficially, since I confessed my feelings to her in 9th grade and she surprised me by confessing her reciprocation for those feelings, but officially after graduation when we both came out to our parents, then announced the relationship online. *How'd they take it?* My parents seemed to take the news okay at first, but they stopped answering my texts and accepting my calls. Her parents were a little surprised at first, but if anything they loved her more for opening up to them. *Have you been to this place before?* No. *If we look through your phone, will we see an incoming call from Miss Nguyen?* Bea, and yes, I don't know. *Miss Bloom, what are we going to find if we discover Bea's campsite? What aren't you telling me? Did you hurt Bea?*

I stopped answering his questions then, but that didn't stop him from asking them. What I didn't tell him was that I wasn't sure what we would find *when* we discovered your campsite, not if, but I knew for certain you wouldn't be there. I knew that it was violent, and that it probably hurt beyond comprehension, but that I didn't hurt you. I didn't know exactly what did, didn't know if we as a species have the capacity to acknowledge exactly what took you or what happened, but I knew that I was the only one that could get you back, even if it meant I would almost certainly die trying.

Still following your wordless directions, we pulled into the entrance of the state park. Your white corolla was the only car in the parking lot, and I quickly jumped out of Reynold's still moving car. He shouted, throwing the car in park and scrambling after me, but I didn't wait up or listen. There was no moon, and it was pitch black and pouring, but Reynolds and the other officers had already caught up to me, illuminating the way with powerful Maglites. Not that I needed the light; with you soundlessly guiding me, I could have gotten there with my eyes closed.

Through the entrance of the park we went, having to go in single file thanks to the thick foliage on either side of the path. The sound of the pouring rain was muffled slightly thanks to the dense canopy above, sounding like a never-ending drumroll. I followed you through the moderately steep trail for about a half mile, my feet squelching loudly in the mud, but knowing where each root, rock, and snag in the trail was, never stumbling once. I could hear the officers behind me slipping and cursing and muttering under their breaths close behind me, but they were irrelevant.

A small part of my subconscious was screaming at me to turn around. That this was stupid, that there was no way you could be gone because you just couldn't be. That you had to be okay, and that taking the police on a wild goose chase in the middle of the night in a state park I'd never been in was probably the stupidest fucking thing I'd ever done, but I didn't give in to that voice, didn't give it an audience. As crazy as it was, I knew what I would find, and I knew that I had to be the one to find it. I owed that much to you, and so, so much more.

I didn't stop, even though my muscles were burning from the excursion and the blisters on my feet had blisters; I kept walking. Detective Reynolds did his best to keep up, still hurling questions and threats and accusations my way, but still I kept going forward.

We came to a fork in the trail, and I hesitated briefly, but you showed me a third trail, the path having overgrown from misuse and almost completely hidden by thick leafy branches. I barreled through, Reynolds and the other officers yelling at me to wait up but still I didn't listen, so urgent was my desire to see where you last stood on this side of reality. The path was brutal, whip-like branches lashing my skin and tearing at my clothes. It was almost like nature was rebelling against my advance, like something didn't want me to go any further, but I fought through, kicking and tearing and biting and wrenching my body through, until I finally stumbled into a large clearing, the sky clear and full of brilliant, radiant stars faintly illuminating the area. Never have I seen so many stars in the sky, but not only that, there was not a single cloud in sight. Where had the rain gone? What was this place?

Your tent was in the middle of the clearing, rippling in a faint breeze, and I stopped, feeling you leave me, the pressure in my head lifting all at once. Without you with me, giving me strength, I started to crumble on the spot. I fell to my knees. Small stones cut into my skin but I barely felt them, for as the wind shifted, an overpowering coppery scent blew in my face, the finality of it making me cry out.

I screamed as Detective Reynolds and the other officers caught up to me, and I didn't stop for what seemed like hours. My voice quickly gave out, turning to an inhuman croak, and I stared as the officers illuminated your campsite, giving a wide berth around the area so as to avoid the blood and preserve the crime scene.

Detective Reynolds was running around with his gun drawn, looking at his phone in confusion and ordering the other officers to try to call for backup. All four of them took out their phones, then their radios, all of them mirroring the same almost comical looks of confusion. They all started talking and arguing at once, but I didn't catch what they said. Their voices sounded warped and distant, but the sound of the tent flapping in the breeze sounded clear even though it was several yards away.

At some point I stopped crying, and I lay there on my side in the dirt, muttering unintelligibly to myself, begging you to come back. I couldn't do this without you. Couldn't live, wouldn't. I refused. All this blood? How could you still be alive after losing so much blood? It was everywhere, semi-coagulating puddles still soaking into the hardpacked dirt of the clearing. It was unnatural, overwhelming, and I imagined I could see particles of it suspended in the air, the whole clearing tinted in a crimson fog.

4

Sometime later, people wearing white Tyvek suits, who I presumed to be crime scene analysts, arrived and placed dozens of placards around the area marking evidence. I was still lying on my side in the dirt, Detective Reynolds crouching beside me, trying to question me, but it was easy to drown him and everyone else out. Sound carried differently here, as if we were under water, the area suspended in a strange, dreamlike stasis.

I was drifting off, exhausted from the night's events, my senses shot, when I suddenly became aware of a new presence. At first I thought it was you, but instead of a flitting form in my periphery, it felt as if something inconceivably large was looming over me, countless eyes burning into me. Its arrival didn't bring me the comfort and clarity that you gave me. Instead, an overwhelming terror gripped me. No, this wasn't you, and more than anything I just wanted to run away, my mind rebelling at the *wrongness* of it all, but my body wouldn't respond.

I felt a strange probing sensation behind my eyes, and my

ears popped as if I was driving through the mountains. My nose started gushing blood, and my arms flopped feebly in the dirt as I tried to staunch the flow, but my body wouldn't respond to my mind's commands and the blood quickly started pooling on the ground beneath me. I began to panic, focusing all my will to get my body to respond, but all I could manage were a few pathetic twitches and jerks.

I calmed down as best I could, closing my eyes and breathing deeply through my open mouth, thankful that I wasn't lying on my back or else I would've probably choked on the blood, when suddenly the activity and sounds around me started to fade, Reynolds's voice tapering off into a deep monotonous drone. All at once I felt my mobility returning to me and I quickly scrambled to a sitting position, blood from my nose now cascading down the front of my shirt and into the waist of my pants. I tried then to staunch the bleeding, but all I managed to do was soak my hands and stop the flow slightly, but then I was spitting and coughing as the flow was diverted to run down my throat. I let my hands fall back down to my sides, looking at the world around me in awe.

I took in my surroundings, surprised that I could see the endless constellations of the clear October sky through Detective Reynolds's body. All around me, I looked to see the world had gone still and transparent; the other officers, your tent, the surrounding trees, even the ground beneath my feet and the stars in the sky were fading, being replaced with something that was difficult for my mind to comprehend. It was like looking through a funhouse mirror, or those glasses that simulate drunk driving. My vision was clear, but the edges of the world were blending together, forming new shapes and colors I'd never seen, ones that strained my eyes if I looked in one place too long.

My head suddenly felt like it was in a vice grip, my nose still streaming red, and I knew that I was experiencing the same thing you did in the moments before you were taken. The world around me continued to fade, the colors fading to a dull grey until everything was just gone, like I was sitting in a great expanse of nothing, suspended in an embryo of dead space.

I became aware of frantic movements in my periphery, and the feeling of icy fingers hooked in my brain, latching on, rooting around in my inner being, analyzing me, readying to consume me, salivating with a hunger that could never be sated. There was a deranged gibbering, still faint, but growing louder as the world around me continued to darken.

I closed my eyes, not trusting myself to not look. I knew in that moment that if I did turn to look upon whatever it was, it would not dart away like you did. It would be the last thing I would ever see. My mind would simply snap at its enormity, at its endlessness, and it would rip me from this world like it did you.

Suddenly, you flashed across my vision, giving me a momentary calm, and the dead world shifted around me in a brilliant, blinding pulse of humanity and color. The Thing screamed in my head and the icy fingers turned into claws, viciously tearing through my subconscious, my mind howling, revolting at this inhuman assault, my nose shooting twin geysers of blood. The world was coming back rapidly now, Detective Reynolds shaking me and screaming my name, asking me where I went and what the fuck was happening, his voice rising to an unnatural pitch in his panic. There was movement from the other crime scene techs and officers all around me, the ground solidifying beneath my prone form. My nose stopped bleeding all at once, and with an audible *pop* the sounds and smells of nature and the world around me returned to normal.

I looked about in a daze and thought I saw a glimpse of what took you, something incomprehensible in its expansiveness. Something impossibly old and all-knowing, all-encompassing in its intelligence and hunger. The other world might have faded, but the unvetted raw terror remained and I was screaming again, repeatedly ramming my head into the bloody earth until I mercifully passed out, the outline of what I had seen following me into the darkness.

5

I awoke three days later in a hospital bed, blinding white fluorescents above me, my arms strapped protectively to the rails of the bed, and Detective Reynolds asleep in a chair beside me; I expected to see your shadow, but you were still gone. I looked around frantically, searching for you everywhere, the heart monitor beeping in response to my panic, but I knew you weren't here. I couldn't feel you anymore, that strange sensation gone from my head, and without it, I felt hollow. Completely empty and alone. I started ripping the electrodes off my chest and an alarm went off. Detective Reynolds tried to calm me down and a few nurses came running into the room just as I ripped out the IV in my arm.

I left against the advice of the hospital and despite Reynolds's protests, not listening to anyone. He drove me home, asking questions that I didn't even attempt to answer. *You said that you had gotten a call from Bea, but her phone was in her car, with no record of having called you or anyone else. How do you explain that? How do you explain knowing exactly where Bea was taken, even though you had supposedly never been there before? How do you explain all the blood? There was no evidence of any footprints other than Bea's in the area. What aren't you telling me Miss Bloom? Whatever happened, I will help you through this. Please.* He had begged. We were almost to the house at this point, and without thinking I turned to him, interrupting him mid-sentence, and told him everything I knew.

I told him that you came to me the night you were taken, instructing me on what to do and where to go. Told him how when I came to the clearing, you left me and something else took your place. Something awful, something ancient, something ravenous. I told him I was afraid you'd be gone for good unless I got you back. He had pulled over at this point and was staring at me, his eyebrows raised, the corners of his lips downturned, his eyes searching my own, as if he pitied me. I had no use for his pity.

Instead, I started asking him questions. How could he explain the absence of my footprints at her campsite? Where was Bea's body? How could he explain the way my nose bled? Did I fade away for a moment, or perhaps disappear entirely? He had asked where I went, I was sure of it, what did he mean by that?

He didn't say anything, pulling off the highway and focusing on the road. A sweat had broken on his brow, and he looked uncomfortable, maybe even afraid. We were both silent the rest of the ride home. When he pulled into our driveway, I got out without another word and went inside, where I decided to rest until night came, and I then would go back to the clearing.

The waiting was the worst part. I tried laying down but couldn't calm my mind, and I didn't want to risk sleeping in case you came back. So, I spent the day walking aimlessly around our house, which was much too quiet and lonely without you in it. I looked through my phone at the endless pictures and videos we had taken together, reliving each moment but looking up frequently just in case I missed you. I had hoped that if I waited until night, you would come back, but the sun had set a few hours ago and you were still gone. At twenty minutes to midnight, I couldn't wait any longer, and I ran out the door to my car.

6

I was unsurprised to see Detective Reynolds's car trailing far behind me as I drove to the state park. I suspected he would have me followed, but I didn't think he would be doing it himself.

I pulled into the park and got out of my car, closing the door and flinching at the sonic boom sound it made in the near silent night. The trees were a vague, menacing outline ahead of me, like giant gnarled figures urging me away. I imagined I could see something shifting in the murky darkness, something menacing. Suddenly, I felt a hundred eyes on me and could feel hot breath on the back of my neck. Sensing a presence behind me I whirled around, teeth bared, but there was nothing.

I turned back around, staring at the dark outline of the woods, and took out my phone and thumbed the flashlight icon. The phone's light didn't penetrate the darkness very much, but I felt better. Holding my phone out in front of me and clenching my jaw, I entered the state park.

I stood at the trailhead for a moment, waiting impatiently, until finally Detective Reynolds's car pulled into the parking lot with its headlights off. He quickly got out and peered through the driver side window of my car. I turned away, feeling less afraid with him close by, and headed up the trail.

Even without you guiding me, it was pretty easy to find the clearing; there was police tape lining the trail most of the way there. At the fork in the trail, the middle path that was initially hidden had been widened. There was more tape and evidence placards lying about. I wondered if this was still an active crime scene but didn't dwell on the thought much. I didn't care. I needed to get you back, and just focused on putting one foot in front of the other.

I came into the clearing cautiously, expecting to see your tent still flapping lightly in the wind, but of course the police had taken it, as it was evidence. The area was deathly still and quiet, and the intense impression of being watched returned. I felt a prickle in my brain and was elated thinking that you had returned, but the sensation passed, and I was left feeling emptier than ever.

I tried to will you back into my mind, hoping you'd return like that first night. The smell of your blood still permeated the area, and the ground was stained a blackish red, giving the dirt a perpetually wet look, as if the earth too was unable to let you go. I stared at the endless stars in the sky and then at the remnants from the crime scene left in the area, frowning in concentration, my eyes straining from the effort, but nothing happened. I waited until the sun started to rise, the world around me waking up as the dark began to recede, and then left. I would come back the next night and each one after, as long as it took to bring you back.

A week passed, then two, then three. I went back to the clearing every single night, Detective Reynolds trailing me the whole time, but nothing happened. I was starting to fall apart. I was barely eating. I hadn't showered since I came back from the hospital, my hair matted and my skin gritty and greasy. My teeth felt fuzzy from lack of brushing. Your parents and friends kept calling and texting and there were frequent knocks at the door, but I ignored them all.

My yearning for you was like a physical pain. I missed everything about you, and constantly, obsessively, looked for your shadow everywhere I went.

I missed your touch; the way you would hug me or touch my face or comb through my hair with your hands, massaging my scalp. I missed the way you smelled; the expensive aluminum-free deodorant you used smelling faintly of baby powder and lavender. I missed the sounds you always brought with you. You were always singing a song or tapping out a rhythm or saying nonsense words to yourself. I'd always thought I was destined to be alone until you came around, but now I was unable to function by myself.

7

I had almost completely given up hope that I would ever bring you back. I convinced myself that I imagined the whole thing, that you were never with me in the first place, that some maniac had attacked you and that you were buried somewhere in the state park or held in some psycho's basement. I was still going to the clearing nightly, but it was more out of habit, for lack of anything else to do, until one night, three days ago, something finally happened.

I had gone out to the clearing as usual. Lately I'd taken up the habit of sitting next to the outline your blood still made in the hard-packed earth, drawing circles in the dirt, staring blindly ahead at the place your tent was, or up at the infinite stars. Every now and then I felt the presence of something sinister, or thought I saw the form of something monstrous in the dark of the night, but I hadn't felt or seen anything for a week and a half or so.

I was sitting in the dirt and humming your favorite song when suddenly I sensed eyes on me, burning into every inch of my body. I heard a noise, sounding like the fabric of your tent flapping in the wind, except there was no tent, no wind. I felt those icy fingers slip into my head, a sense of dread overwhelming me. My nose started sputtering blood and a series of horrible images filled my head the same way as when you disappeared. They were nightmarish scenes, horrible hellish tableaus that triggered my fight or flight and threatened to snap my mind in half with their outlandish awfulness:

Millions of people burning alive in liquid fire.

An impossibly large tendrilled claw shearing through piles of stacked bodies.

A blood drenched mouth filled with millions of foot-long razor sharp teeth obliterating mountains of flesh and gore.

Endless huddled forms floating in gray oblivion, suspended in nothing and unmoving, Bea among them.

A closeup of your face, withered, your eyes turned to black coals, the skin around them charred, your mouth yawning open unnaturally.

Many more unspeakably horrible stills flashed through my head like a flip book from hell, but none of them were as devastating as seeing your beautiful face turned hideous in death. You looked like you died in terrible pain, your face forever frozen in an endless wail of utter agony and despair.

I started as I noticed an unnatural keening. I looked around wildly, but then realized the sound was coming from me and that I couldn't stop. I would never stop screaming and seeing the horrible things that awaited me if I stayed here. I could no longer see Bea's shadow because she was dead or dying or something much worse, and if I didn't leave this place for good, I'd be next. But what was the point if Bea was no longer here? What kind of life could I live without her?

I continued to wail, something bursting in my throat and hot blood coating my dry mouth. I wanted to be taken too. At least then this torment would be over. With that thought, I became aware of an insane warbling noise, followed by an all-consuming tearing, as if the fabric of the world itself was being wrenched apart.

I closed my eyes and screamed, awaiting oblivion, welcoming it, not stopping to catch my breath or when I felt someone grab my shoulders. All at once the presence left me, and I collapsed to my knees, spent, my screaming turned to body-wracking sobs. I felt strong, warm arms embrace me, and I didn't fight it, couldn't. My eyes were swollen almost completely shut and were burning fiercely from crying, my throat filled with needles and ripped ragged from my cries. My stomach and back muscles spasmed painfully with each ragged intake of breath, my lungs burning from each exhale. Detective Reynolds didn't say anything, just crouched there with his arms around me as I cried myself to sleep.

8

When I awoke it was morning, the sun shining warmly upon me, the nature around me lively and comforting. I was alone. But no, there was Reynolds at the edge of the clearing, sitting in a lawn chair, arms crossed over his broad chest, his chin resting on his chest, sleeping. Seeing him there I felt a pang in my chest, of guilt or shame I'm unsure. I looked up, noticing clouds in the sky and birds flying overhead. I had never been here in the daytime, but somehow it made perfect sense that it would be peaceful with the sun out.

I didn't see the point of spending any more time in the clearing now that I knew what became of you, and so I went home in a haze. I spent the next three days in a stupor, staring blankly at the walls. The days and nights passed in a blur, no single moment discernable from the next or the one previous. I daydreamt of you, of all the places we went and the things we did, and of all the things we have yet to do. I thought about the image of your dead body and if it was true, or if it was a warning of some kind. Was this what would happen if I didn't stay away, or what had already happened? When I did sleep, it always ended in a fitful thrashing that shook me awake soon after nodding off, those nightmarish images becoming more twisted in my dreams.

I was debating on how long I wanted to go on like this when I received the call from Detective Reynolds. The search for you had officially ended. I asked what that meant, and he said essentially there would be no more police funding put towards finding you. They would still follow up with any leads that came through, but without a body, footprints, DNA, or any discernible evidence other than the blood that was determined to be yours, they didn't have anything to pursue. He paused, then asked if there was someone that could stay with me, a hint of worry in his tone.

It's been two hours since I hung up on him, and I've made up my mind.

Tonight will be the last night. I would bring you back or I wouldn't, but tonight it would be over. I would stay at the clearing until I was taken, like you. If I somehow managed to find you and you were alive, I would try to bring you back. If I couldn't, then at least I would be with you. I would die in the clearing and be with you eventually in whatever comes next.

I packed a bag to prepare for my last night. A blanket and pillow, a thermos of Sleepytime tea with a handful of sleeping pills slowly dissolving inside, and last but not least, a wickedly sharp straight razor. If I wasn't taken, it made sense to go out this way. I'd sit in the middle of your campsite, admiring the endless stars and constellations, chugging the warm tea. When I started to feel sleepy, I'd take the razor and open myself up, my blood mixing with yours, now long dried and leeched into the earth.

I felt a strange pressure in my head, and imagined I saw a shadow flicker in my periphery and spent the rest of the day wandering around our home looking for it, waiting for night to fall, calm now that my decision had been made.

THE LAST HIKE

"OHMYGODLOOK!" Michael screams, raising his camera's view finder to his eye and pointing it to the canopy above. "A red-breasted nuthatch!!"

I scan the treetops, not really caring but wanting to keep up the impression that I do. I can see a small brown form flitting away, looking like every other small bird we've seen on this godforsaken hike in the woods.

Michael lowers his camera. "I think that was actually just a sparrow, but still pretty cool right?" I make the appropriate noises, but he is already turning away, dead leaves and twigs crunching beneath his feet as he jogs a few yards ahead on the overgrown nature trail.

"Fucking Christ," I mutter under my breath, increasing my pace to catch up to him before he disappears. The last thing I need is to be lost in this lush hell, where I'll probably die, slow and painfully, starving to death. Come to think of it, it would take a special kind of dumbass to get lost on a trail like this. Yes, it's twenty miles, but it's literally one giant circle. Perhaps I would get eaten by a bear instead?

Are there bears in Ohio? My anxiety spikes for a second as Michael rounds a curve in the trail and I lose sight of him. *Whatever.*

I hate my boyfriend, have for quite some time now. Well, maybe hate is too strong of a word, because there are times when my heart feels so overcome with love that my chest aches, and sometimes, I'm certain it will quite literally explode, but those times are getting fewer and farther between. I'm not even quite sure how it started, but one day the same eccentricities and oddities that made me fall in the love with the oddball, kind-hearted man that is Michael became the same qualities that I now resent.

I can't count how many times I've worked up the nerve to finally leave him, only to chicken out at the last second, convinced that we can rekindle the burning love that has since been reduced to mostly ash this past year. Well, I shouldn't say *we*. As far as I can tell, Michael is completely unaware of my internal struggle, blissfully ignorant of my ever-growing annoyance and irritation. I feel overcome with guilt and stop walking, feeling the sudden burn of tears stinging my eyes. Michael's going to be devastated if, no, *when* I finally cut things off.

The thought of breaking Michael's heart causes a black hole to open up in my chest, threatening to swallow me whole. But staying with someone just because you're afraid of upsetting them is stupidly selfish. Michael deserves someone who will love him unconditionally, quirks and golden retriever energy and all. I angrily rub the tears from my eyes, calling for Michael to wait up.

My body is covered in a thin sheen of sweat, my shirt already soaked even though we're only ten miles in. I slap a mosquito dead against my arm for the five hundredth time, my whole body feeling like one giant itchy welt. I feel like I'm completely covered in seeping bites and bug guts. I swing my backpack around on one arm, rifling through its meager contents, but of course the bug repellent is in Michael's pack.

I open my mouth to call out to him, but accidentally inhale a mouthful of gnats, temporarily choking me and turning my stomach. *This was a mistake*, I think bitterly, my irritation coming back with a vengeance.

I should have let Michael come on this trip alone and packed my stuff while he was away for the day. The house is in Michael's name, there are no pets to fight over for custody, we each have our own gaming systems and TVs, our own books; it would be an easy break. Now that I think about it, I really don't know why I agreed to go on this trip in the first place.

Maybe just so you could tell yourself in the future that you really tried your best? That makes sense. The truth is, I really don't understand my animosity towards Michael a whole lot. But I'm hapless to change it, and every day it grows stronger.

Our story is nothing special. We met five years ago on a dating app. I swiped right because he was nice to look at, not because I saw a long term committed relationship with him. We went on a few dates, the first at a bar, the second at a bowling alley, and after the second date I went back to his house and planned to have a one-night stand because I only *ever* had one-night stands.

I have a number of self-harm scars, mostly on my arms close to my shoulders and some on my thighs, but there are a few other clusters scattered about my body. Ever since I was a young boy, I always hated how I looked. I've been an angry person my whole life, but my self-loathing knew no bounds, and there were times in my life when only harming myself would bring me peace. The cutting tool didn't matter. I used pencil sharpener blades, razors, chef's knives, scissors, sewing needles, and one time, a beautifully sharp piece of obsidian that caught my eye at an herbal store; anything that draws blood I've probably tried at one point or another. The urge still arises every now and then, but thankfully I've been clean for about seven years now.

Unfortunately, the scars remain, serving as a constant reminder of the lowest points in my life and creating many awkward conversations between potential love interests. I never thought I would have any sort of committed relationship, but I still craved human affection every now and then. So, I would jump on a dating app, swipe right on anyone that didn't look too uppity, and pray for the best. We would meet at a bar, get absolutely shit-faced, go back to their place (always their place), and then have stupid, drunk-sloppy sex that I would barely remember (with the lights off, and with me as fully clothed as possible). Then I would sneak out as soon as they were asleep and call myself an Uber home. I never gave anyone the chance to comment on my scars and had convinced myself that I would live this way until my libido ran out.

But Michael was different. From the start, I could tell this wasn't going to be like my usual flings. Michael was way more attentive than I was used to, and he wasn't drinking as much either. It seemed like he was really trying to get to know me, which freaked me the fuck out, and so on our second date I decided to get drunk enough for the both of us. The rest of the night was a blur, and I awoke in his bed the next morning, the rising sun shining in my eyes through the half-opened curtains, wearing clothes I didn't recognize, with Michael sitting up and reading a book beside me. I was just trying to formulate an escape plan, kicking myself for losing control, when he turned toward me, a huge, goofy smile on his face, looking absolutely delighted to see me.

He said, "You got pretty messed up last night, but don't worry, we didn't do anything. You *did* get sick all over your clothes though, which was gross, but I washed them before going to bed and they should be dried now. So, what do you wanna do today?" I was uncomfortable at first, feeling awkward for being such a mess the night before, but I quickly discovered that Michael and I shared a genuine connection, one I didn't fully acknowledge while shit-faced. We ended up spending the whole day together in his apartment just talking and enjoying one another's company, and I felt genuinely happy for the first time in a long, long time.

Before I got my hopes up too much, I decided to be up front with him about my scars, but Michael's reaction surprised me. Instead of acting weird, he had laughed and said, "Uhhhh yeah, I noticed them when I was cleaning the puke off of you, but I could tell they're older for the most part." He had paused, thinking. "Nothing new, right? You're not suicidal?" He paused again, then smiled, asking, "Homicidal?"

I did my best to explain that the last time I cut was about 2 years ago. That I was never seriously suicidal; the cutting was some bizarre coping mechanism that I barely understood myself. And that the thought of causing harm to another person made me physically ill. When I asked if it bothered him, a confused frown on my face, he just shrugged, saying simply, "We all have our shit."

Two weeks later, I was leaving a toothbrush and a change of clothes at his place. Four weeks after that, I had moved in. And now here I was, kicking myself for having wasted so many years of our lives. We're both twenty-nine, and now we're gonna have to start over from scratch. Better late than never, I suppose. I take a deep breath of the suffocatingly hot and humid August air, trying to calm my nerves.

Get your shit together Jared, man up. You can ruin Michael's life when you get back to the car, where there's AC, but first you have to make it through this hike. And look there, mile marker eleven. Only nine more miles to go. Can you at least try *to enjoy yourself? Would that actually kill you?*

I take another deep breath and feel better, calmer. It would be an awkward, uncomfortable hour-long car ride home, but I felt my resolve hardening now that I could see an end in sight.

The faster you rip the band aid off, the faster both of us can move on and find the people we were meant to be with in this life.

This relationship wasn't fair for either of us.

I can see Michael up ahead, fumbling with the settings on his camera, and whatever he is looking at must have flown or scampered away because suddenly his body droops in an almost comical expression of defeat. Looking at him, bent over, camera dangling dangerously close to the ground, arms hanging limp, I feel another debilitating wave of sadness overtake me.

Is this how he will be moping around the house in my absence? Can you really live with yourself knowing that you completely broke his goofy, beautiful soul?

But then he suddenly righted himself, jerking his body upward, but overestimating and he stumbled backwards, falling heavily on his ass.

The momentary sadness washes away so quickly it is like it was never there. It is replaced by the annoyance and irritation that has been my near constant companion these past few months.

Through painfully gritted teeth I call out robotically, "You good?" and hurry my pace to catch up with him. He looks up as I'm a few steps away and says cheerily, "Yeah Jare-Bear, I'm great!" He shoots his hand out and I grab ahold and haul him up, steadying him as his feet wobble, afraid he might fall again. My hands are still on his shoulders, and I notice him smiling lovingly at me. It turns my stomach as a familiar wave of self-loathing washes over me. Even dirty, sweat-drenched, and covered in about as much bug guts as me, Michael is still annoyingly attractive. He has a high and tight haircut that he gets touched up every two weeks and a mustache that only he could pull off. His eyes are brown and intelligent, always gleaming with humor or mischief. He's as tall as me, about five foot ten, but he has broad shoulders and is well-built thanks to a strict workout regimen and hiking every free moment he has.

I force myself to look away, my face reddening with exasperation and embarrassment, and ask, "Before you run off again, can I get the bug spray out of your pack? I'm being eaten alive. And it's Jared, you know I hate Jare-bear."

"Oh yeah sure thing, sorry babe," he says, smiling sheepishly and turning around. I unzip his pack and grab ahold of the can of repellent. I'm just about to zip it up again and tell him I like "babe" about as much as "Jare-Bear" when he gasps loudly and runs ahead, camera pointing somewhere in the distance, totally ignorant to the fact that his pack is still open and its contents are falling out on the trail.

"Wait–damnit. Michael hold up!" It's no use. He is in the zone, hellbent on capturing whatever he had spotted with his battered old Nikon and oblivious to the fact that his loud charging probably already scared whatever it was away.

Sighing heavily, I swing my pack around on one arm, open it up, and retrieve all the items that Michael dropped in his haste: his sunglass case, a rain poncho (god what I wouldn't do for some rain right now), a foldable hunting knife, three granola bars, a warm bottle of water, and lastly, sticking out of a patch of mud and sporting a new crack I don't think was there before, is his cellphone. I zip up my bag, not seeing Michael ahead of me and wondering where he ran off to. I wipe the muck of his phone and as I'm about to put it in my pocket I feel it vibrate in my hands.

I look at the lit-up screen absentmindedly. I'm about to call out to Michael again but I stop, seeing a text message notification from someone named Gar. I can't see what the text says with his phone locked, but as I'm searching my memory for anyone that we know of named Gar (short for Gareth maybe? Garchomp, perhaps?), Michael's phone starts ringing in my hand. This time I do call out Michael's name and answer the phone, but before I can say hello a deep, gravelly voice interrupts me.

"Thank fuck you answered baby. I started thinking about you during a team call and got so fucking hard. Did you get my picture? Can you facetime me?"

I stop dead in my tracks, anxiety forming a pit in my stomach. *What the fuck?*

He must have misread my silence, because he quickly adds, "Oh shit are you with Jared? I can call you back later, it's just been too long since I've seen you and it's driving me fucking crazy."

An abyss opens in my stomach, threatening to consume me. I take the phone away from my ear and look at it stupidly, then back up at the trail, seeing Michael nowhere in sight. *Have I been played? Am I a complete fucking idiot?*

I feel both faint and furious. Like I might either pass out or explode. This whole time I've been debating on leaving, has Michael been off fucking around with someone else? Is this some kind of joke? Or is Michael really cheating on me? The thought never seriously crossed my mind. Sure, I would get a pang of anxiety whenever he wouldn't respond to my texts or calls right away, but I never *seriously* thought that Michael was anything but one hundred percent devoted to me and our relationship.

My blood starts to boil picturing Michael with another man. Probably laughing at me behind my back the whole time. Lord knows he'd have plenty of opportunities to be seeing someone else. Michael works in HR for a huge insurance company and has been working from home since the pandemic, but he still goes into the office for meetings and to file documents. Pretty much every other moment of free time Michael has he is outside, taking pictures of anything that moves. He drives all over the state looking for new parks and areas to explore. *Supposedly. For all you fucking know he could have been meeting up with* Gar *or whoever the fuck.*

I come crashing back to reality, realizing that Gar is saying something else. I cut him off mid-sentence, gathering my courage and swallowing back the lump in my throat. "Yeah Gar, this is Jared, and you know exactly who I am so let's cut to the chase. Tell me, how long have you known Michael? Where did you meet? How long have you two been fucking?"

Heavy breathing from Gar's end. The momentary kick in the gut feeling is now totally gone, having been replaced with white hot anger. "Oh, I'm sorry, did I deflate your hard on? My apologies, just wait a second let me fix that for you, I'll get Michael now. But while we wait, please do tell. How long has this been going on? I'm *dying* to hear the details."

Unintelligible babbling from Gar now, and I can't help but laugh. "God, I really am stupid huh. Come on you fucking coward, you can at least man up and answer my questions. How long?"

After a long pause there's an "I'm sorry" and it sounds like he's stifling a cry. I laugh again as the line goes dead, and then suddenly I can't stop. I'm laughing harder than I can remember ever having laughed before. I hunch over, unable to catch my breath but unable to stop, laughing at my stupidity, laughing at the irony of it all. This whole time I've been killing myself over my decision to leave, and Michael's been cheating on me probably the entire time. I'm still laughing, my stomach muscles starting to cramp, and then suddenly I'm crying, hot, stinging tears streaming down my face. I drop Michael's phone and now I'm really out of control.

I fall heavily to my knees and pull my hair, slap myself in the face painfully. "Stupid stupid stupid!" Each word is punctuated with an ear-ringing slap. The whole world is spinning, and suddenly I just want to hurt myself. I think about the knife I picked up, now in my backpack. I imagine the reassuring click as I open it. It would probably be very sharp, and I can imagine how it would part my skin like butter, the trenches in my flesh standing in stark relief and bloodless for just a few seconds before starting to well up and run over. Then I would repeat the process again, and again, and again, until I started to feel like a person once more. I take a deep, shuddering breath and feel a little better, my tears drying up but my face red hot and raw from my slaps.

I look up at the trail and Michael is still nowhere to be seen. He's probably still chasing after whatever it is he thought he saw. I laugh again and shake my head. *You haven't lost control like that in years. Probably good to let it all out, but Jesus man get it together.*

I feel spent and decide I'm just going to wait here until Michael notices I'm not following and comes to look for me. I briefly debate whether or not I should confront Michael, or just say fuck it and go ahead with my plans to break things off at the car. *This would definitely make things easier, but...*

No, I need to know the extent of Michael's infidelities, then I'll confront him. I grab Michael's phone and crawl over to the edge of the trail and lean up against a tree. The lock screen pops up, and I input the pin number that Michael uses for everything: 4321. I half expect it to not work, but it does. I pull up Gar's unread message and am greeted with a dick pic and a winky face emoji. My blood starts to boil again as I realize that this is real, not some sick joke, and it boils even more as I scroll back through their messages, my stomach full of knives.

At first, it's more or less what I was expecting. Gar would typically initiate, either with "You alone" or just throwing caution to the wind and sending various nudes from a number of locations. In one it looked like he was outside in the woods, another in what looked to be a porta-potty, another in a changing room at some store. I was surprised at the number of times Michael responded with his own nudes and surprised even more at how many times he was the one to initiate. I can't think of a time when we *ever* sent this kind of stuff to one another, even when we first started dating. I was struck by how vulgar, and, well, *kinky* Michael was. I didn't recognize the almost feral messages he sent back and forth.

I start to scroll faster, my vision beginning to blur, not paying attention to the pictures and the occasional video, just wanting to see when this first started. I stop when I notice a picture unlike the others, and I scroll back to read the accompanying lengthy text, the saliva drying in my mouth and a dull, throbbing headache forming at my temples. I scroll to the beginning of the thread and start reading, my breath catching and more tears starting to sting my eyes. I get to the end of the paragraph Michael sent and read it again, my lungs constricting and panic starting to take over again, my heart shattering.

Michael: Gar, you have no idea how bad he gets. I would leave him right now if I wasn't sure he would slit his fucking wrists the moment I ended things. Not like that would be any big loss, but I don't think I can live with his blood on my hands. I finally snuck a picture so you can see what I mean. Its fucking disgusting. I shit you not, I gag every time I see them and have to hold back puke every time I touch them.

I see the picture that made me stop scrolling. It's a photo of me lying on my back in bed, only in my underwear. The keloid scars on my right arm and thigh are visible, looking ugly and pale pink in the dark room. I click on the photo and see that it was sent around five months ago. I try to think back that long to remember if I felt like Michael was acting strange or different at all, but nothing is coming to mind. I feel oddly removed from my body, staring at myself, trying to see what Michael sees.

It took me a while, but finally I became comfortable

enough with my own body to be shirtless around the house, and eventually, even in public. It was a big mental hurdle to convince myself that Michael didn't actually mind my scars and loved me in spite of them, maybe even because of them. Regardless of how I felt about them, they made me who I was. But apparently his acceptance was just another deceit. The thought of Michael secretly being disgusted with me is almost too much to bear. I have no idea what he meant about "how bad" I can get, though. Sure, I get depressed every now and then, but I have never gone off the deep end or done anything that would warrant Michael to feel that way about me.

But really, how could you know? Clearly, Michael is not the man you thought he was. How will I ever recover from this betrayal? I had wanted to move on from Michael so we could both be with who we were meant to be with, but now how can I ever trust anyone ever again? How can I ever feel comfortable in my own skin, ever again?

It's almost as if I'm having an out of body experience, and I can't really get a read of what I'm feeling. *Probably shock.* I tap out of the photo and read on.

Michael: See what I mean? I have to see them just about every single day and it's just disgusting. I honestly feel like he's proud of them, like he's happy he fucking ruined his body. I've seriously been looking for an out for months now, but I'm just trying to think of the best way. In a perfect world, he would leave me, but I don't think that will ever happen. Just give me time baby. You know I'm crazy about you, I haven't felt this happy-

"Jared?"

My heart jumps out of my chest, and I snap my head up, my neck cracking from the sudden movement. Michael is standing about ten feet away on the trail. He's holding his hands out in front of him, as if he's trying to calm a wild animal.

"Oh, hey Michael," I say, sounding nonchalant. "Just catching up on some reading. What's up?" I scroll down a bit to one of the countless pictures of Gar's dick and hold the phone out to him. "Interesting stuff for sure."

When I see Michael's terrified expression – face white as a sheet, mouth agape, eyes bulging – I could almost laugh. Or I could rip his face off. Or, and this one felt most likely, I could stay sitting on this trail for the rest of time, leaving my body for the wolves or bears or whatever the fuck prowls these woods.

"Jared," Michael repeats, but then says nothing more. His eyes are darting back and forth from his phone to my face, as if he's trying to think of a quick explanation or excuse but is coming up short.

"Please don't embarrass yourself with cliches like 'ohmygod it's not what it looks like, please believe me.' Also, don't try to blame me for not trusting you and looking through your phone. You're a bastard. I hate you right now and probably always will, but I'm just done. I want it over, and it looks like you do too. Let's just go home. I'll start moving my shit out as soon as we get back and you'll never see me again. I also promise not to kill myself or go crazy, so no worries there. Sound good?"

Halfway through my speech, Michael's mask of terror gave way to sorrow, and now he's full-on sobbing. He takes a few lumbering steps closer to me and falls to his knees only a few paces a way. Still crying loud body-wracking sobs, he clasps his hand together as if in prayer and looks me in the eyes, tears and snot streaming down his face.

"Jared. Love, please don't leave me. You've gotta believe me, I've been trying to cut things off with Gar for weeks now. I fucked up, I'm not gonna lie, I fucked up bad." I snort loudly, looking at him incredulously as he goes on. "But if anything, that just made me realize that I'm meant to be with you. We're meant to be together. You can't end things now, not when I've realized I fucked up. Please Jared, please. I'm begging you. I can't live without you."

I laugh ruefully, venom lacing my voice, "I can't leave you huh? You should have thought of that before you fucked another man. Sorry, repeatedly fucked another man. He's hot though, didn't see a single scar on him, you guys would make a great couple."

"I didn't mean anything I s–"

"How long?" I interrupt him. "How long has this been going on? How'd you meet this *Gar*? I didn't get that far in the messages before you interrupted me."

Talking slowly, cautiously, he says, "I met him at a work event. Remember the holiday party they threw around Christmas last year?" I nod. "Well yeah, it was there. We hit it off pretty much right away, and before we got split up by other coworkers, he gave me his number and told me to call him sometime. So, I did, and I guess you know–"

"How often," I interrupt again.

"How often what?"

"'How often what'" I mock, spitting the words at him. "How often did you meet to fuck. Once a week? Twice? How often, and when was the last time?"

He pauses a beat, then says, "At first, we would just meet for lunch any time I had to go into the office. But then things just got away from me, and we were hooking up pretty much anytime, anywhere we could. Which I know is bad, but you've been so, just, fuck! So unavailable! So uninterested. I know you have your issues and I tried to be there for you, but it's like you're always so annoyed! Even during the height of it when Gar and I were meeting every chance we could get, I always tried with you. I *always* tried to be there for you. Tried to talk to you, be there with you and for you, but it was like you'd always rather be somewhere else! Even now, when I'm trying to make you understand you're giving me a thousand-yard stare. I mean fuck, Jared!"

He is pacing back and forth now, alternating between waving his hands wildly in the air and running them through his hair.

"Are you done?" I ask, stifling a yawn, but also trying to hold back my anger and tears. "That was quite the speech, but I meant what I said." I stand up and underhand toss the phone in his direction. It hits the ground with a muffled crack, but Michael makes no move towards it and continues pacing back and forth. "I'm done. You're right, I've been distant recently and all that yadda yadda, but now I'm just done. Believe it or not, I've been trying to work up the nerve for a while now to leave you, and this trip was going to be my last try to make things work. To make my feelings towards you change. Our last hurrah. Because you wanna know what Michael, my dearest?" I ask sweetly, mockingly.

He's standing stock still now, searching my face intently, as if trying to catch me in a lie. He hesitates, then asks, "What?"

"I cannot FUCKING STAND YOU!! It must have been a subconscious thing on my end, because around the time you started your little affair, I was checking out. I never went off and fucked someone else, that's where you and I differ completely as individuals. I could NEVER do that. But yeah, if you wanna know the truth, everything that makes you who you are as a person just fucking drives me INSANE!!" I scream the last word, drawing it out into an unintelligible roar. Michael takes a step back, hands raised in the air as if he wants to cover his ears.

I continue, "I'm not gonna get into the details, you aren't worth the time and energy for that, but I think this is for the best. Yeah, it's *definitely* best that things end this way, so now I don't have to spend the rest of my life missing you or wondering where things went wrong. No, I'm sure I'm probably just as wrong for our relationship not working out, but you fucked up and fucked someone else. Worse than that, you talked shit about me? Made fun of the way I looked to some brain-dead dipshit asshole? Yeah, I've got my issues, and maybe if you'd just fucked the guy, we could *maybe* move past this, but no." I pause, breathing heavily, trying not to think about the disgusted, hateful way he talked about me. Michael is crying in earnest now.

"Whatever. What's done is done. Now and forever, I can spend the rest of my life hating you. You will always be the man that cheated on me, the man who betrayed me, and that's it. I'm honestly surprised you're not happy about this. Now you can be free to go fuck who you want. Or did you only like Gar when you were with me? Like a package deal? Never mind, don't answer that. Let's go and get this over with. If we hurry, we can probably get home before it gets dark, and I can start packing."

I start walking in his direction, to the end of this godforsaken trail, and when he doesn't move I shoulder check him out of my way. "I'm heading to the car," I say over my shoulder. "Come or don't, but I'm leaving."

"Jared–fuck, Jared please wait!" Michael sobs.

I ignore him and keep on walking. *I can't fucking believe him. Should I be flattered that he wants to still be with me? Or that he supposedly wanted to end things with fucking* Gar?

I walk on, trying my best to ignore him.

The miles pass slowly by. Way too fucking slowly. Michael cries and begs basically the whole time, but the more he mopes and pleads, the easier it is to ignore him entirely.

At around mile marker fifteen (five miles to go) he starts running ahead of me and falling to his knees dramatically, begging and crying hysterically. I pass him without paying any attention, and then he runs up ahead and repeats the process. It really is almost funny, in a pathetic way. Funny that he thinks he deserves my forgiveness.

Thankfully with the bug spray I haven't had to deal with the bugs. I didn't bother offering Michael any, and he's starting to look pretty bad, but serves the fucker right. I drink most of my water and eat the granola I find in my bag. At one point I'm going to ask if Michael has any snacks in his bag, but I notice with a start that he not only doesn't have his bag, but he must have lost his camera during his dramatics as well. I think about mentioning it because I know how much Michael loves that old thing, but really, I just don't care at this point. My only regret is I wish I had kept ahold of Michaels phone. A big part of me wants to continue reading the messages that Michael and Gar sent back and forth, to see what else they said about me, but maybe it's best if I don't know. I pull my phone out of my pocket for the hundredth time and press the power button, but it's still dead.

As we pass mile marker nineteen, and I can *just* see the curve that marks the final leg of the trail, Michael runs in front of me, again, only when I try to push past him, this time he puts his hands on my shoulders and restrains me, physically holding me in place, a crazed look in his eyes. He really does look like shit. His face is flushed bright red, and almost every available inch of his skin is covered in angry looking bug bites. His knees are red and raw from repeatedly falling on the trail. His nose is running, his lips cracked with dried spit gathered in the corners of his mouth. He's shaking almost uncontrollably, and he's somehow still crying. His eyes look puffy and deeply bloodshot, the pupils dilated to pinpricks.

I shrug him off and hand him the rest of my water.

"Drink this, you're gonna die of heat stroke."

"Fuck that," he says, batting the water bottle away and causing it to fall to the ground, spilling its meager contents.

"Jesus, Michael what the fuck? I would've–"

"Forget that!" he shrieks. "I don't want water. I don't want food, I don't want air, I don't want to live! I only want you!"

"Oh my god Michael, really? Don't be corny. You should've thought of that before you fucked around. Let's go". I remove his arms from my shoulders, feeling exhausted deep in my bones, and start to brush past him again for the hundredth time, but Michael doesn't give me the chance.

"NO!" he roars, enveloping me in a bear hug and squeezing me impossibly tight, constricting my breathing.

"Michael," I choke out, my voice sounding muffled as my face is smashed against his chest. His skin feels fiery hot through the fabric of his shirt. He lifts me off my feet and leans back, somehow squeezing me even harder, my ribs straining under the pressure, my lungs burning fiercely and I'm barely able to take a breath. My arms pinwheel uselessly against his broad shoulders and back, and my feet bat weakly against his shins, causing him to squeeze even harder. Black spots fill my vision, and I'm filled with the certainty that if I can't get away, Michael will suffocate me into unconsciousness, maybe even kill me.

Without thinking, I suddenly stop resisting, going limp in his arms. I slip a few inches, still in his grasp but now my feet are touching the ground. Quickly, before he can get a better grip on me, I bring my knee up swiftly to his groin. He groans, dropping me hard. I land on my hands and knees, and I waste no time in crawling away from him. Small stones and sticks cut into my hands, but I'm too panicked to feel them. I take a deep breath of hot, humid air, my lungs burning and my ribs pinching from the effort. Michael's shadow falls over me and I look up, cringing at the alien look of fury clouding his face. He towers above me, blocking out the sun, making him look even more physically imposing. His hands are clenched into white knuckled fists, powerful muscles rippling under his skin.

Looking away and sitting up a little, I swing my backpack around on one arm and quickly start rummaging through it, looking for the hunting knife Michael dropped earlier.

He rips the pack away from me, the zipper of the bag catching the webbing of my thumb and tearing the skin there a little, and he turns the contents out onto the trail. It seems like we both see the knife at the same time. I lunge for it, but I'm quickly stopped when Michael's hiking boot connects solidly against my chest, the air whooshing out of me. He follows up with another vicious kick to my side, a sickening cracking noise and sharp pain letting me know one of my ribs is broken.

I gasp, breathing shallowly, painfully, lying curled in a protective ball on the trail. I've never been in a fight before and am shocked by the sudden bout of violence.

"Michael, what are you–" I rasp, trailing off, looking up at Michael and feeling a cold sweat pinprick my whole body.

Gripped in his right hand is the hunting knife. With a loud *CLICK* it's open. He's holding it out at me, hand shaking, the 6-inch-long, serrated blade looking very sharp and very dangerous.

"Looking for this?" Michael asks, his eyes wild, a deranged smile on his face.

"Michael," I say weakly, holding out my hands in surrender and standing with an effort, my whole-body trembling. "Put the knife down. Please."

"NO," he bellows furiously. "No you're gonna listen to me! We are going to talk like a couple, and we are going to work this out. We're not moving ONE MORE STEP until we figure this out! I love you, and I know you love me. Let's work this out and move on together, okay?"

"No," I reply simply, shaking my head.

"No?" he asks, looking perplexed.

"Yes Michael. I mean no, no we are not going to work this out. Look at yourself. Look at me. You attacked me, you fucking kicked me." I pause, staring over his shoulder in complete bafflement, shocked that things have gotten so crazy. I continue, "Now you're holding me at knife point? What are you gonna do, fucking stab me? Kill me? No, we're leaving. Let's just forget that all of this happened and let's go."

I move to walk past him, hunched over in pain and putting pressure on my injured side, not really thinking he will attack me again. As soon as I brush by him I stumble back, feeling an icy hot slash across my arm. I take a few more faltering steps backward and look at Michael, stupefied. He looks as confused as me, staring at the knife still gripped in his hand, now coated red.

I hear a staccato tap-tapping sound and look down to see an impossibly long, impossibly deep horizontal slash in my right arm near my shoulder. The edges of the cut look ragged and almost crumpled from where my scarred skin was bisected by the serrated blade, and the arm of my shirt and skin are both hanging in shreds. There's no pain yet, it tingles more than anything, but blood is sheeting down my arm and soaking my shirt at an shocking rate. I look a little closer and can see pale yellow bubbles of fat in the center where I'm cut deepest, almost to the bone, gnats already alighting on the gaping wound.

I look up to see Michael staring at my arm, transfixed. His hands raise in surrender, but he is gripping the knife and bright red blood drips down the serrated edge. He's still within stabbing distance, and without thinking I quickly shoot my uninjured arm out and punch him as hard as I can in the face. With a loud snapping noise Michael's nose breaks and blood flies. Without waiting to see how he'll react, I turn and run as fast as I can towards the exit. My hand is pressed to my injured side, and I'm trying to breathe through the pain. With each pump of my arm, I can feel my wound flex open wider. I grind my teeth, trying not to focus on the feeling. Glancing quickly down, it looks like I just dipped my arm to the shoulder in a bucket of red paint, but I can't focus on that now.

"Wait no, please! I'm sorry!" Michael cries, his voice muffled and slightly garbled, and I realize he's somehow already following close behind me.

I feel in my pocket for my keys and my phone and thank God they're still there. I just have to get to my car, then I'm leaving. *Then what? Wait for your phone to charge then call the cops? FUCK!*

Up ahead, maybe a quarter of a mile away, I can see the trail curving left. After that, it's just a short distance to a small clearing at the beginning of the park with restrooms and informational signs, and beyond that, the parking lot.

I risk a quick look back and see Michael (way too fucking close) behind me and getting closer. He looks completely crazed. His eyes are flaring and rolling wildly in their sockets. His nose is pointed at a skewed angle, blood streaming from both nostrils, the red-coated knife in his white-knuckled grip.

Something's broken inside of him. You just need to get out of here, and quick before you lose too much blood.

With that thought comes a wave of dizziness, and black spots fill my vision. I try to take a deep breath, but I can only manage insubstantial, shallow intakes, my broken rib feeling like its stabbing me directly in the lung. I bite my tongue hard, a coppery taste filling my mouth, the sharp relief of fresh pain focusing me.

I run on, the surrounding woods a blur in my periphery. I'm starting to lose steam and Michael is within grabbing distance, sounding like a wild animal. I imagine I can feel his hot breath on the back of my neck, and I push on, feeling myself on the verge of collapse.

Just as I finally reach the curve in the trail, I slip in a patch of mud. I comically wave my arms to keep from falling. Instantly Michael is upon me. He doesn't stop, knocking the air out of my lungs as he hits me from behind in a flying tackle. I fall in the mud on my side with a splat, my teeth rattling and my shoulder twinging in pain as its stretched from its socket. I hear Michael crashing somewhere off the trail to my right with a rustle of leaves and snapping branches, and he lets out a sharp cry before falling silent. I try to get up and away, but I'm moving slow and can't seem to catch my breath, my broken rib continuing to stab. I hear Michael groaning.

I plant both hands on the muddy trail, lungs burning and head woozy. I'm thankful I didn't land on my injured arm, but it's still bleeding freely. I look over and see Michael a few yards off the trail, still standing but leaning heavily against a pine tree and covered in mud from his tumble down the edge of the trail. I shakily stand and take a few unsteady steps forward, now standing directly in front of Michael and noticing the knife stuck in his chest.

Somehow, during his fall, he must have landed directly on it, and the wrapped plastic handle of the blade is stuck to the hilt about two inches to the right of his sternum. He looks up at me dazedly, blood trickling from both sides of his open mouth and still streaming from his broken nose.

He looks like he's trying to say something, but what

comes out instead is a wet garbled noise, accompanied by a fine red mist spraying from his lips.

Oh shit, he's fucked up bad. I start to panic and take a tentative step towards him, but then stop as reality comes crashing in and I remember what he's done to me, what he will still surely try to do to me if I get near him.

"Oh Michael," I say, a wave of sadness washing over me, the stress of the day's events finally catching up to me. "Don't touch the knife and don't move. I'm gonna go to the car and wait for my phone to charge, then call for help."

Michael makes like he is going to follow me, then groans in pain and sinks back against the tree. His hand reaches tentatively towards the knife handle, but as soon as he touches it his whole face goes white as parchment and his eyes turn wide and glassy.

"Fuck–Godamnit! If you wanna fucking bleed to death, keep moving around like a dumbass, but if you want to live just fucking stay there and don't move! Fuck!"

I don't know why I care. Afterall, he's already tried to kill me twice within a short time frame. My emotions are all over the place: I'm tired, sad, pissed off, and scared, but a big part of me doesn't want Michael to die. Even if he wants to kill me, the thought of having his blood on my hands is just too much for me to bear.

I tear my eyes away from Michael's pathetic form and turn towards the exit, jogging as quickly as I can, wanting to get to the car soon so I can call for help.

I have only been running for about thirty seconds and am just rounding the final bend when I see two men about a thousand feet ahead, turning right at the beginning of the trail to start their own hike.

Relief floods over me. Finally, this will be over.

"Guys!" I scream, my voice sounding hoarse and

unrecognizable. "Hey guys, help! We're hurt and need help. Can you call someone?"

They turn around, and I can just barely make out their confused faces.

"Help!" I scream again. "Call 911! We need an ambulance. My boyfriend's been stabbed and my arm is all fucked up. Please!"

They confer with each other for a second, clearly unsure of what to do, and I'm just about to fall to my knees and wail when they start jogging my way. I do collapse on my knees then, falling hard and sending a jolt of pain up my thighs, but I don't care. This will be over, finally. I can move on from this fucking nightmare.

As they get closer, I can see they both look to be middle-aged with deep tans. They're tall and well built, and I feel comforted knowing that they'd probably be able to best Michael if he somehow gets his second wind. They're wearing matching white shirts and yellow shorts, but the man on the left is wearing a blue baseball cap and the right is wearing an orange bandana. Blue Hat pulls out his phone but hasn't called yet, and Orange Bandana is digging through his pack for something. He takes out a frayed looking towel and jogs up to me, eyeing my arm with concern.

I imagine how I must appear to him. I glance down at my arm, which is tacky from layers of half dried blood, the right side of my shirt completely sodden with it. I can feel a weak flow of blood still leaking from the wound, but I don't have it in me to look at it again. I stupidly, self-consciously wonder if he can see the scars on my injured arm, but I think there's probably too much blood and gunk for him to make them out and I settle down. He holds the towel out to me, and I take it, pressing it hard to my wounded arm, gritting my teeth through the pain and a fresh wave of dizziness.

Orange Bandana asks, "What the hell happened? You

said your friend's been stabbed too?"

"Yeah," I say, not bothering to correct him. "He's just right up there, off the trail. Thank God you guys were here." I look over to the Blue Hat, who's still holding his phone with an indecisive look on his face. Anger blooms in my chest. "Look at me, you should be calling from how fucked up I am alone, but I think my friend might be dying. He has a knife in his chest."

Orange Bandana snaps his head from my arm to my face, scanning me as if he thinks I'm lying. He apparently doesn't see any deceit on my face, and he looks back to Blue Hat and says, "Go ahead Joe, call for help." Joe nods and dials quickly, putting the phone to his ear but shakes his head after a few seconds.

"Ain't got a signal. I'll run to the parking lot and see if I can get one there. I'll come back as soon as they're on their way. You good with this?" He raises his eyebrows and looks pointedly at me, making me feel guilty even though I've done nothing wrong.

Orange Bandana nods and Joe jogs away towards the parking, not looking back. I sigh, feeling relief once again. Right now, a light breeze could knock me over, and my arm is starting to throb with every beat of my heart. I don't give myself a moment to rest even though I desperately want to. Michael might have lost his mind, but he still doesn't deserve to bleed to death. "This way," I say, walking back to Michael. "He's just right over here."

"What's you and your friend's name?" he asks, falling in step beside me.

"I'm Jared, he's Michael."

"Okay Jared, I'm Dean. You wanna tell me what happened to your arm and how Michael got a knife in his chest?"

I hesitate, feeling his eyes burning into the side of my face. "It's a long, stupid story, but maybe you'll hear me tell it to the cops when they get here."

"All right," he says, not sounding placated in the slightest but willing to let it go for now.

We both round the corner and I jog to the edge of the trail to see Michael lying on his back in an ocean of red, the knife missing from his chest. His chest rises and falls rapidly, and he's looking around wildly. He's doing nothing to stop the bleeding, which is pumping at an alarming rate from his chest wound with each beat of his heart. Instead of trying to staunch the flow, his hands are on either side of his body, rooting around in the shallow puddle of his life's blood. I'm unsure what he's doing at first, but then it comes to me.

He's looking for the fucking knife!

"Michael!" I scream, running full tilt down the slight incline. Kneeling in the ever-growing puddle of his blood, soaking my shorts and shoes but not caring, I quickly remove the half-sodden towel from my arm and peel off my completely sodden shirt, cringing as it brushes against my half coagulated wound and restarts the bleeding in earnest. I crumple both my shirt and the towel into a ball and press it hard against Michael chest.

He breaths in deeply and moans, a bubble of blood escaping his lips. His eyes meet mine, and I'm surprised to see he still looks furious. He bares his red stained teeth at me and gives an inhuman growl, more blood bubbling out from his mouth.

"Oh fuck," Dean yells himself, his voice cracking. "JOE, IF YOU CAN HEAR ME, TELL THEM TO COME QUICK. IT'S BAD."

"OKAY," we hear Joe yell in reply seconds later.

Dean stumbles loudly down the embankment. "Oh

fuck," he moans softly. I turn around, still trying to stop Michael's bleeding, but both the towel and my shirt are already soaked through. Michael's hot blood runs through my fingers as if I'm ringing out a wet sponge. Dean has gone almost as pale as Michael, staring transfixed at the ever-expanding puddle of blood surrounding us. The ground has turned into a red, coppery smelling swamp.

"Throw me your shirt," I demand, and when he makes no move I add, "Now!"

My voice snaps him out of his trance, and he complies, peeling off his shirt and throwing it to me.

I catch it with one hand, my arm drenched in fresh arterial blood to the wrist. I pause for a second to throw my sopping-wet shirt and towel to the side, hearing them hit the forest floor with a wet *SPLAT,* and then I'm placing Dean's shirt over Michael's wound. I groan in frustration at how fast it gets saturated. He must have cut something vital when he ripped the knife out. Michael would not be making it out of these woods alive.

I tear my gaze away from his chest and look him in the eyes again, seeing my own desperation mirrored there. He looks terrified, absolutely terrified, and seems to understand the severity of his situation. I feel an unexpected wave of anger pass over me and tears sting my eyes.

"You motherfucker," I cry. "You're going to fucking die and it's all your fault. Why? Why did you do this? Why couldn't you just let me go? Why did you pull the knife out? Fucking why!"

I'm really crying now, out of control again, unable to stop. I'm vaguely aware that Dean has kneeled beside me, his large hands pressing over mine, trying to help slow the bleeding, but it's pointless. I feel Michael's body hitching beneath my hands, and I look down, thinking he must be in some death-spasm. "Oh Michael," I sob. "Mi–"

Michael starts flailing his arms wildly. I look at him, trying to settle his seizing. I shriek wordlessly, desperate for this nightmare to be over, but suddenly my breath is knocked out of me as Michael punches me hard in the stomach. I cry out as I feel a deep, searing pain in my gut. Michael has stopped his thrashing and is looking directly at me, an insane look of fury on his blood-drenched face. Dean must notice something's wrong, because I hear him say "Jared?" and feel his hand on my back.

I look down to see that Michael plunged the knife to the hilt into my midsection. With that realization comes more pain, somehow both white hot and piercing cold at the same time, and I fall backwards. Michael still has a hold of the knife though, and it slides free of my stomach with a sickening slurping sound, followed by a torrent of blood. I fall on my back and cover my hands over the wound, feeling hot wetness pump through my fingers and across my torso, forming my own ever-growing puddle of blood.

That bastard. That fucking bastard. You should've left him for dead.

"What the–" Dean starts but is cut short. I look up in time to see Dean take three large, lumbering steps back before he falls with a crashing thud. The ground seems to shake from the impact, and Dean makes a wet gargling noise.

Still feebly holding my wound, I raise my head enough to see Michael lying motionless, the knife still in his hand. Dean is a few yards away on his back, blood spurting wildly from a second mouth that has opened up in his neck. He's been cut almost from ear to ear, and I look away as I see him trying in vain to stop the bleeding, hands clumsily groping at the gaping, gory maw and causing himself to bleed out quicker.

Steeling myself, I press my hand to my stomach as hard as I dare, gritting my teeth so tight I'm certain they'll shatter, and slowly crawl over to where Dean now lays still, wading through a lake of muddy blood, leaves, pine needles, and other debris floating in the warm liquid. As I get closer, I can see he's already dead. Dean's eyes are open and glassy, his mouth agape, his once tanned skin now looking gray and almost translucent. The blood from his neck has slowed to a trickle now that his frantically dying heart is no longer beating.

He must have been so scared. He probably has a family too. People that depend on him. What a fucking waste.

I feel the anger that has been my near constant companion these past few months come back with a vengeance, giving me strength. I take my hands from my gushing wound, not caring if I bleed to death, only needing to put all of this to an end. I stand up, groaning as the hole in my stomach stretches open and blood pumps out in a flood, but I can't worry about that now. I take five, stumbling steps towards Michael, my shoes squelching loudly through the bloody swamp. I almost slip, but I manage to catch myself at the last moment.

I tower over Michael's prone form. He still has the knife gripped in his hand, and he looks up at me lazily, a ridiculous smile tugging at the corners of his bloody mouth, a snot bubble of blood forming at his broken nose.

Without thinking I drop my knees on Michael's forearm and cringe as I hear the sharp sound of his arm snapping in two and his subsequent gurgled cries. I rip the knife from his useless hand and crawl over his body, digging my fingers in his flesh.

I straddle him, both of my knees planted in the bloody muck on either side of him. We're both completely soaked head to toe in red, our bodies glistening in the shaded light of the woods. I don't hesitate. Still straddling his body, holding him in place, I grip the knife in both hands and raise it above my head, my stomach wound yawning wide open. I bring the knife down as hard as I can, right where I imagine Michael's heart should be.

Time seems to slow as the knife plunges downward in the moments before it pierces Michael's heart. We lock eyes, staring at each other for a moment that seems to stretch on forever. I think about the shit show this day has become. I think about how much I loved this man, and how I don't anymore; I can say that with absolute certainty. I mostly just feel pity for him. I want to think that this dying lunatic beneath me is not the same Michael I fell in love with, but really, how can I be sure? I had no idea he would be capable of betraying me the way he did, and I can't help but wonder: was it always going to end this way? Would Michael ever have let me leave? There's so much going through my mind, and it's getting hard to think with all the blood I've lost, all the blood I'm still losing. But I know one thing for certain: even if I live through this, I will never be able to sleep at night with Michael's blood on my hands. He might have thought I was the crazy one, and maybe I've done some crazy shit, but as much as I've hurt myself throughout my life, I'm not a killer

At the last moment, right before the hunting knife plunges

into his chest for the second time, I jerk my arms to the left, and instead of piercing Michael's fucked up heart, the blade makes a

squelching noise as it lodges to the hilt in the blood-saturated ground beneath us. Michael had closed his eyes, scrunching dramatically as he awaited his execution, but I gently slap him in the face and he looks confusedly up at me, his eyes asking the question his mouth can't manage: *why?*

"Sorry about your arm," I say, returning my hands to the gaping wound in my gut. I groan as I shift my weight off Michael, pivoting my leg so that I land on my ass in the swampy earth. I remove one bloody hand from my stomach and press it as hard as I can manage to Michael's chest wound, making him groan but stopping the weak flow as best I can. I can see his arm is canted at an odd angle and the skin is discolored. "Oh god, really sorry, but I didn't want you stab me again, you fucking asshole." I feel the annoying sting of tears burning my eyes, but I quickly blink them away. "Joe should be coming back with help soon, and I think you should live through this so you can explain to him and the cops why his friend is dead. It shouldn't be long now, I'm pretty sure I can hear the sirens."

They're still faint and far off, but it's definitely sirens I hear. I close my eyes, willing them to hurry up so this can finally be over. All I want to do is go home, but I guess I'll probably be heading to the hospital along with Michael. The more I think about it, the house I shared with Michael is no longer my home. How can I ever step foot in that house again without reliving this day and all the horrible things that happened?

I'm starting to nod off from the combination of exhaustion and blood loss when I hear movement nearby, and seconds later Joe comes running down the embankment, almost slipping in all of our blood. He takes a second to scan the scene, taking in the nightmare around him, and then falls to his knees next to Dean's corpse, starting to cry.

"Dean!" he wails, leaning over to puke loudly, retching as his stomach heaves until there's nothing left to come up. I feel overcome with emotion, Joe's grief breaking me. If I didn't ask for their help, then Dean would still be alive. Even though I'm not the one that landed the killing blow, Dean's blood is on my hands. I look down to see that Michael's head is turned away from me, his eyes rolled back into his head, his mouth open in a rictus of death.

I start crying too then, overwhelmed with grief, pressing both hands as hard as I dare against my gut again, Michael's blood mixing with mine, when I hear Joe charging towards me. I catch one glimpse of his face, insane with grief and fury, before he grabs me under my armpits and tugs me violently away from Michael's body, carrying me a few feet before throwing me hard up against a tree, my head cracking against the wood.

"WHAT HAVE YOU DONE?! WHAT THE FUCK HAVE YOU DONE?!" Joe shrieks, flecks of his spittle tapping against my face. The world is spinning now, everything going dark and blurry around the edges. I understood how it looks. Joe probably thinks I killed Michael, then lured Dean here and killed him in cold blood.

"It's not what it looks like, it wasn't me. Michael stabbed me and killed Dean as we were trying to help him. He went crazy and I'm sorry, but you have to believe me." Or at least that's what I tried to say, but I'm pretty sure it came out in long, unintelligible groan, my head swimming.

Joe rears back and punches me hard in the face, my head snapping violently to the right, a tooth breaking free and shooting down my throat. From my elevated position against the tree, I can see what used to be Michael. Flies have already started to alight on his corpse. I did not go through all of this to get beaten to death by Joe, so when he rears his hand back for another punch, I lean my head to the side. Instead of hitting me square in the face he only lands a glancing blow across my cheek, his knuckles crunching as his fist grazes my face and then slams against the tree.

I quickly get to my feet and run back towards the trail, giving it everything I've got. I'm halfway up the embankment when Joe tackles me from behind, his arms wrapped around my waist. I scream, trying to shake him off, but it's no use; I've lost too much blood, and Joe is too furious, convinced that I'm a murderer. The sirens are loud and close, and I imagine I can see flashing lights, but I can't be sure.

I scream "HELP! HELP ME! HEH–" but am interrupted by Joe grabbing the back of my head and repeatedly slamming my face into the ground. With the last of my strength, I push off on my hands and knees, causing us both to tumble back down the embankment.

We land in a heap back where we started, Joe moaning beside me. I feel bad for hurting him, but it's a fleeting thought. Everything is fading quickly now, and I scream internally, cursing the world for this spectacularly shitty day.

I can still faintly make out the sound of sirens wailing nearby, and I think I can hear movement on the trail above, but that is far away. Unimportant now. Everything is fading to black, and it's a relief to feel nothing. I'm so exhausted. I've been so unhappy and so angry for so long. It will be good to rest.

What moments before sounded like sirens, now sounds more like a bird's call. I wonder what kind it might be. Maybe a red-breasted nuthatch?

ACKNOWLEDGEMENTS

First and foremost, many thanks to Ben Long, my editor on this project. Thank you Donnie Goodman, for designing the cover. Thank you to my fiance, Sebastian, for being the first person to ever lay eyes on these stories and for always encouraging me. And thank you to all my followers, and everyone in the horror community that has supported me and followed my journey as both a horror content creator, and now, a horror author! You're continued support means everything to me. Thank you.

Manufactured by Amazon.ca
Acheson, AB